Straight?

Also available by Jack Hart
from Alyson Books

The Day We Met

Heat

My Biggest O

My First Time

Straight?

True Stories of Unexpected Sexual Encounters Between Men

Edited by Jack Hart

alyson books

LOS ANGELES • NEW YORK

COVER PHOTOGRAPHS BY JOHNATHAN BLACK.

MANUFACTURED IN THE UNITED STATES OF AMERICA.

THIS TRADE PAPERBACK ORIGINAL IS PUBLISHED BY ALYSON PUBLICATIONS INC.,
P.O. BOX 4371, LOS ANGELES, CALIFORNIA 90078-4371.
DISTRIBUTION IN THE UNITED KINGDOM BY TURNAROUND PUBLISHER SERVICES LTD.,
UNIT 3 OLYMPIA TRADING ESTATE, COBURG ROAD, WOOD GREEN,
LONDON N22 6TZ ENGLAND.

FIRST EDITION: AUGUST 1998

02 01 00 99 98 10 9 8 7 6 5 4 3 2 1

ISBN 1-55583-475-2

LIBRARY OF CONGRESS CATALOGING-IN-PUBLICATION DATA

STRAIGHT? : TRUE STORIES OF UNEXPECTED SEXUAL ENCOUNTERS BETWEEN MEN / EDITED BY JACK HART.

ISBN 1-55583-475-2

1. GAY MEN—UNITED STATES—SEXUAL BEHAVIOR. 2. HETEROSEXUAL MEN—UNITED STATES—SEXUAL BEHAVIOR. I. HART, JACK.

HQ762.U6S73 1998

306.76'62—DC21 98-23657 CIP

◆ Contents ◆

◆ Introduction ◆

What gay man has never lusted after a straight counterpart? It's both our blessing and our curse that so many men who are so desirable are so distressingly off-limits. That inaccessibility may be at the root of the attraction, and the angst that accompanies such unsatisfiable longing may at times be exquisite, but on the whole it's still not an easy lot to swallow.

Sometimes, however, fortune throws us a bone in ways we can scarcely imagine. Every so often one of those unattainable objects of desire turns out to be not quite as straight as we thought. Sometimes they're open to experimentation. Sometimes they're closeted or bisexual. And every once in a while they're the so-called "straight-acting, straight-appearing" type that so many of us seek, a homosexual who speaks the masculine language of the straight and can walk effortlessly among them without fear or deception.

It's not about fear or deception for these men, not about repressed homophobia. They are who they are, often open and proud but simply not obviously gay, even to the trained eye. In this collection of short erotica, written by some of the finest gay authors working today, love-struck men who love men discover that things are often not what they appear. That jock, that frat brother, that swaggering coworker may actually want into your pants as badly as you want into his.

There are lessons to be learned in these pages that will serve every practicing homosexual well: Don't prejudge, because looks can deceive. Don't give up, because you never know what might happen. And never, ever close your mind to any possibilities, because life—fickle, fanciful, and frequently feral—will always keep some surprises up its sleeve.

Jack Hart
August 1998

◆ Aide and Comfort ◆

My short career in the military was spent mostly in the closet, though not from lack of opportunities. Although not a daily occurrence, other soldiers made their attractions known to me—from the artistic captain who invited me to one of his art openings to the tall, dark, definitely handsome enlisted man who openly invited me to his bed. But discovery and a dishonorable discharge were fierce motivators in keeping my libido in line.

I let my sexual armor down only once, and then only because I fell in love.

The object of my ultimate affections was not someone who initially attracted me. I was his wife's friend more than his. He and I worked in the same cushy headquarters office and commuted in the same carpool. But of the carpool occupants, I was more attracted to Jim, a nerdy but lantern-jawed Army accountant. Andy seemed too flashy, too scrawny, too sure of himself to need my attentions.

But one day the telephone rang. Andy's voice told me between sobs that Ellen, his wife, had left him. She had gone home to New Jersey, taking their baby daughter with her. I didn't feel too sympathetic toward Andy. He struck me as the kind of guy who would have been voted most likely to cheat on his wife and had in our daily dealings long since turned me off with his superficiality and sexist comments. He was the commanding general's aide and awfully full of himself.

Before I could stop myself, though, I asked, "Why did you call me?"

"Who else could I call?" was Andy's answer. That was such a sad thing to hear, especially given my opinion about him. I resolved to be nice to him for the duration. But that didn't prepare me for his next question: "Can I come over?"

It was early evening, and I hadn't eaten dinner, but I kept my resolution. "Sure," I said, then added, "Have you had dinner?" I bit my tongue too late.

"No," Andy replied almost cheerfully.

After I hung up, I cursed myself. I didn't like the guy. I would probably be hearing from Ellen soon with her side of the story and would undoubtedly side with her. *Oh, well,* the angelic side of me sighed, *it's only dinner.*

Andy arrived with a big bottle of wine and a big smile. So much for grieving over the end of a perfect marriage. But as I cooked and he drank and we ate, I could hear how upset he really was and how vulnerable he felt. His self-confidence was shaken, and my image of him cracked.

I listened to Andy for hours while he drank and talked and cried. Staring at the dark hairs on his wrist, I noticed that his watch said it was almost midnight, and tomorrow was Tuesday. I decided I'd better drive him back to his place. Then he looked up at me with velvety brown eyes, set off by bushy black eyebrows, and said huskily, "Can I stay here tonight?"

My sexual armor shot back up immediately. "I can drive you home."

"I don't want to stay there tonight," he pleaded. "I don't want to be alone."

I took a long look at him. He tried to look back at me, but, drunk as he was, his eyes kept wandering. Our eyes didn't lock, and there was no look of sexual recognition, so I said OK. He slept in my bed, and I slept on the couch. Or rather, I tried to sleep. After he came out of the bedroom to say good night dressed only in his briefs, my sexual armor disintegrated. He wasn't scrawny at all. Indeed, he was small but well-proportioned with a chiseled chest, muscular thighs, and a cock that showed a lot of promise beneath his cotton Jockeys. I hoped he wouldn't notice my erection.

I felt my sexual dams bursting, but all he did was smile and say good night. I couldn't even jerk off because he left the bedroom door open.

The next morning I was beat, bleary-eyed, and dreading the day. Andy woke me up with the same smile, a happy "Good morning!" and the banging of pans. He was cooking breakfast. All amazement, I tried to stumble into the bedroom for my robe before my hard-on returned. As I rose, he watched me—an appraising look if I ever saw one.

I had plenty to show him. I was six feet tall, 170 pounds, and—thanks to the Army—in terrific shape. Now it was my turn to smile.

Over scrambled eggs and toast, Andy asked if he could stay a few nights. Twenty-four hours earlier it would have been easy for me to say no. Now I couldn't; sex had its foot in the door. I agreed, and Andy hurried off to get ready for work and pack. It was his turn to drive.

At the usual time Jim and I met on the sidewalk to wait for Andy. (We lived in the same apartment complex.) I debated whether to update him on Andy and Ellen, did, and regretted doing so when Andy drove up, who was as insufferably animated as usual. He was even whistling.

As we drove to the post, Andy concisely informed Jim of Ellen's departure. He was brisk. There were no tears. Jim and I stared repeatedly at each other. Neither one of us liked him very much.

That evening Andy drove us back to the apartment complex, parked, and then took his bag out of the trunk. Jim looked at me as if to ask, "What's going on?" I tried to give him a look that said I didn't know. Andy explained, effervescently, of course, that he was staying with me a few nights. Jim replied out the side of his mouth that that would make his commute easier.

Andy stayed for two weeks. We slipped into a nightly pattern of cooking together, drinking, and talking. I learned much more about him and began to like him in spite of myself. He was a shallow, happy, handsome person. It seemed unfair to dislike him so much. I got used to the underwear parades and the looks with no follow-through. He gave me back my bed and slept on the couch. Ellen never called, which made me feel she had abandoned both of us.

After two weeks Andy decided to give up his apartment and move into on-post housing. *That's that,* I thought, *back to normal.* I helped him pack, and a crew of us helped him move some worldly belongings, put the rest into storage, had a beer together, and said good-bye.

That evening I missed him. I missed his company. I missed looking at him and knowing he was looking at me. I even missed his infernal cheerfulness. Thinking of Andy in bed that night, I jerked off and then went to sleep.

The next day Andy called and invited me to dinner at the officers' club. That began phase three of our relationship, a quasi dating that gradually made me hysterical with pent-up sexual urges. It was as if he was courting me or at least cock teasing. He always picked me up. He brought wine and even, one time, flowers. He directed all his attention toward me when we were out together. I was very flattered. I fell in love with him. I thought of him all day long, fantasizing, masturbating when I dared. I wanted it. I wanted him, but he was straight. He called me his best friend, his buddy. Every night ended in sexual frustration for me. Finally I began to say no to his nightly invitations. "What's wrong?" he asked with those puppy-dog eyes. What could I say? I said yes again.

One night he insisted we go to a movie. It was, get this, *Barbarella.* He ushered me into my seat solicitously and sat to my left, on the aisle. There was no one to my right. The theater darkened; the movie began. Suddenly I felt something brush up against my left calf. *Rats?* I wondered.

I stamped my foot. The touch came back, and it was clearly a hand. I froze in my seat. The touch became a caress, a gentle massaging of my calf through my slacks. I relaxed and leaned into the caress. It continued, exploring all of my leg, but surreptitiously so as not to be seen by unsuspecting neighbors. My hard-on began to ache, straining through layers of clothing. I tried not to breathe heavily. I think I was sweating, staring unseeing at the screen.

Andy's voice asked softly out of the void, "Do you like this movie?"

"I have no idea what it's about," I whispered back, my voice cracking.

"Let's go home," he concluded, standing up, his coat in front of him.

Home, it turned out, meant my apartment. We drove in Andy's car, and, atypically, not a word was spoken. Andy's face was set straight ahead. He didn't look at me once, even when I turned to observe him. Somehow his attitude calmed me down. My mind stopped whirling, my breathing became regular. I thought happy thoughts of the erection in my pants and what was to come.

I opened the apartment door with my key, and Andy closed it behind us. I turned the light on; he turned it off. In the darkness he kissed me and put his arms around me. As we embraced, our hard-ons hit, perfectly aligned. I pulled away in surprise. He pulled my ass back, pressing my erection against his, opening my mouth with his tongue, and kissing me in fulfillment of so many daily fantasies.

Our breathing accelerated. He kissed my neck, my chin, my lips. He held my ass in place, moving his cock back and forth across mine. I was ready to come in my pants when he pulled back and silently began to unbutton my shirt, massage my chest, and pinch my nipples.

"You like that?" he whispered into my left ear as he nibbled the earlobe. "I love playing with your tits."

"I'm sorry there's not more," I said with a shaky voice.

"All I need is a handful," he said, his voice low and breathy, and squeezed my chest gently before stepping back and unbuckling his belt. "Take your pants off," he said as he removed his shoes.

In very little time we were both naked. He was several inches shorter than I, and his eyes glistened in the moonlight coming through the curtain sheers. "I like this," he said, taking my waist in both hands and touching the tip of my cock with the tip of his. I held on to his shoulders, the heat of his body burning my fingers.

"Suck me a little," he directed, finding my shoulders and slowly but firmly pushing me down to my knees. I hesitated, but he pushed my head toward him, and I opened my mouth to take the head of his cock, then the length, as he began to face-fuck me. He moaned low and long. "Women never do this," he whispered. He reached down and found my nipples, pinching them as I sucked, the pressure increasing my mouth's pneumatic action, and vice versa, until I yelped in pain. "Sorry," he said, pulling me up to him, hugging my tightly. "Let's go to bed," he whispered urgently in my ear.

Moonlight seemed to fill the bedroom as we entered. I could see him clearly. I wasn't sure he appreciated the light, but he looked me up and down and smiled, throwing back the covers and pulling me down with him, rolling on top of me.

Andy was excellent at lovemaking. He didn't hurry. He didn't just whack off and say, "How 'bout a cigarette?" He squeezed and kissed and rubbed the length and breadth of my body, then centered himself on me, letting his cock rest next to mine while he began slowly to pump both together.

Then he raised himself and looked around the room. "Got any lotion?"

"No."

"I'll use spit."

Lubricated, he shifted my legs to his shoulders, then paused. "I don't want to hurt you."

"You won't," I promised, amused that he thought it was my first time.

He spit once more onto his hand, jerked his cock twice, and held it firmly against my ass. I tilted my asshole up to meet it. It entered and popped the sphincter, sliding easily inside me.

Andy grinned and groaned. "Man, that feels good! I am *so* horny."

I smiled back, happy with the feeling.

We had that one night and no more. We stayed friends, but sex was clearly off-limits. Andy gave me this message via looks and behavior. I got the message and was actually relieved. Having a love affair in the Army seemed even less a good idea than a quick poke once in a while.

Eventually Andy and Ellen decided to reconcile. He was given a hardship honorable discharge and went home to New Jersey while I stayed in the Midwest to complete my service. Through cards and occasional visits, the three of us stayed friends until their divorce, when I suppose I became part of the past they both wanted to put behind them. It was also best for me. I cared for Ellen and felt disloyal that I had loved her husband, not to mention been fucked by him. After their reconciliation Andy reverted to form and made it easy to put that love in perspective. I had been his friend and lover only briefly, out of his situational need. Once his needs changed, I realized I had never liked him very much. Still, some feelings remain, and I remember our moment in time very fondly. Andy is a part of my past I like to keep with me.

R.M., San Francisco, Calif.

◆ Amen ◆

My first sexual experience with a guy happened in, of all places, my hometown church. No, not in the sanctuary (that would really be a story!) but in the basement men's room.

I was 19 and on a football scholarship at a local community college. As a linebacker, I stood 6 foot 2 and weighed 205 pounds of solid gridiron muscle. Girls thought I was hot stuff, but I never managed to work up much interest in them. Oh, I'd date and all that, but the times I'd had sex with a girl were…well, disappointing. I figured someday I'd find what really interested me. Did I ever!

One Sunday morning I went to church and, before the service began, realized I needed to use the rest room. I also figured that while I was at it, I might as well yank my rod a few times too. At 19 you're perpetually horny.

The best place for privacy was the basement men's room. When I got there I saw that the basement was deserted, so I didn't bother to close the door all the way. After a long, satisfying piss, I let my cock hang out of my Sunday slacks. It didn't hang long, though. In no time my meat was hard and ready—all nine inches (not to brag, it's the gospel truth). My right hand gripped the base of my cock and started pumping. About half a minute into this speedy session, the door squeaked open. There stood Mr. Aymes, my best friend's dad. Talk about getting red in the face!

"Mr. Aymes," I stammered. "I didn't know anybody was around." He just laughed, eyeing my hard cock, and said, "Relax, Chris. I get urges too."

Before I knew what was happening, he was on his knees with my rod in his mouth. I'd never felt anything so good in all my life. At first I resisted, but after a while I backed up against the wall and let him suck me dry.

I'm telling you, I had never come so much, so fast! It felt like bucketfuls were blasting down his hot throat. I didn't know what to say after he got me off, so I just thanked him (I was taught to be polite) and got the hell out of there.

Is that the end of the story with Mr. Aymes? Not exactly. His son, C.J., and I became even better friends. So I had an excuse to go over to his house. And when C.J. wasn't around, Mr. Aymes and I would work on his car—with the garage door down. I soon learned it's blessed to give as well as to receive.

C.F., Denver, Colo.

◆ Banding Together ◆

Just as I lay back on my bed and flipped on the TV, he walked into my bedroom. I was already aroused; my cock swelled lazily in my shorts. He sat on the edge of my bed. As each minute passed, I was becoming more intensely excited. I was ashamed of myself for feeling this way in his presence, but I knew that anyone who found himself in his company tended to be overwhelmed and a little intimidated. He's so intelligent, and he acts so superior without being obnoxious or overpowering.

I knew he was strictly for the ladies: Women are the blood of the band, and we brag a lot about our flings with the groupies. The thought of having sex with another man had never entered my mind—not even for a split second.

He and I had always been pretty close—especially when I'd first joined the band. I'd replaced the band's previous drummer, and he had been very supportive and understanding, but we'd never been this close.

"You need a girl," he jeered. His playful tone turned to a more serious one. "Or is it a boy?" He leaned forward and parted my robe at the hips.

My cock, purple and throbbing with lust, stood free of the garment. *Lust for what?* I thought. *Him?*

I was shocked at myself even though I knew it had been a long time coming. I was becoming wild with excitement. I'd always been drawn to him, but I had never imagined we'd express our interest in each other like this.

I felt my balls tingling with excitement as his hands approached my aching penis. I was almost trembling. I secretly wanted him to do whatever he wanted, but then my conscious mind screamed, *Stop!*

"Why are you doing this?" I asked.

He looked deep into my eyes and said, "Because I want to, that's why!"

Why fight it? I thought.

He slapped his right hand firmly around my cock, and I lurched—my nerves wired and ready. I was scared—afraid that I was going to like it too much. His palm began expertly stroking my shaft.

"Yours is bigger than mine," he joked.

"Really?" I replied.

"Sure!" he chuckled. "Show and tell?"

I guess he was trying to make me feel more at ease, but it wasn't working. Here was my best friend stroking my dick. It felt so sexy, though. As he was jerking me, he reached up and untied my robe, baring the rest of my body.

He ran his left hand through the hair on my chest. *No different than a woman,* I thought. *It's sickeningly delicious.*

He gave me a farewell glance as he bent his head to my crotch and inhaled my member. I felt as if my entire body and soul were in his mouth. I took a deep breath and tried not to groan as the intense feelings welled up inside me.

His lips were firmly stretched around my meat, his grip very firm at the base of my cock, and his head bobbed up and down on my shaft. I was going over the deep end. I liked it so much.

A man really does know how to give head better than a woman. He knows how it feels and which parts to stimulate. It wasn't long before I was thrusting into his mouth. He didn't let up; he just stepped up the pace and pressure.

He waited until I began to climax and then squeezed almost too hard on the base of my prick. I was groaning and crying out and thrusting, and he was sucking furiously, his head nodding faster, his fist spasmodically squeezing at the base of my dong. I was begging him to let me come.

The second he released my shaft from his hand, I exploded in his mouth. I distinctly recall hearing myself pleading for him to swallow it; at the time it meant so much to me.

After it was over, he stood up, and I placed my arm over my eyes. I felt a sweet-sour burning in the pit of my stomach. He wanted to say something, but he turned and walked out. After that it was as if nothing had happened.

P.T., Kingsport, Tenn.

◆ Beer ◆

It began as a normal Friday night. I left my office, went home, made dinner for one—the usual. (I've lived with my parents since my separation from the Air Force.) Then, around 10 or 10:30, I decided to hit the local bar—a straight bar.

I put on a pair of jeans and a T-shirt with a sweater over it. I made it to the bar around 11, went in, and stood along a wall, looking around to see if there were any good-looking men among the hordes trying to pick up on women.

In a few minutes I saw him out on the dance floor. He was wearing jeans and no shirt. I looked at his fantastic body, his facial features, dark hair, nice smile, thick mustache. Then I studied how the hair on his chest covered only the upper part of his pecs. From there it trickled down in a hairy little line that went into his jeans and down to a part of him that I badly wanted to see. He danced really wild and was drinking a lot. When he lifted the women he danced with, his arm muscles pumped up.

At last he returned to his table and took a good swig of beer. As the bottle lowered, our eyes met. It wasn't a typical look but a very interesting look. He smiled and slowly made his way through the crowd, stopping every now and then to talk to other people. I assumed this was to build up his confidence. He was carrying his shirt, and as he got near me, he put it on.

I could smell his breath; it smelled of beer. Ever since I can remember, I've been turned on by men with beer on their breath. I felt a nervous anticipation of what the night would bring.

"Hi, I'm Paul, what's your name?" He sounded pretty drunk.

"Nice to meet you. I'm Shane. You from Port Orchard?" I'd never seen him before.

"No, but my girlfriend went to school here. We're visiting her parents." Paul was appraising my body.

"Where's your girlfriend? She here?" I tried to sound as if I were interested in meeting her.

"No, she stayed home with her mom. I'm here with some people I met." He smiled. I thought I'd pass out from the way his lips curled. Little dimples showed on his cheeks. It didn't seem to bother him if people saw how he looked at me, his face just a few inches from mine.

He said he had to go back to his friends but would talk to me later. I didn't want him to leave. I wanted to ask him certain questions I thought he might pick up on.

About an hour passed. Then I saw a friend of mine, Steve, standing by Paul. I walked up to say hello to Steve. Paul began chatting with us. Then the devil entered me, and I asked Paul if he wanted to go somewhere to fuck.

He looked puzzled and asked what I'd said. I repeated the invitation. He asked why I wanted to fuck another guy when the women were all staring at me; he said I could have any one of them. But I kept my eyes on his and told him he was the one I wanted. At that, Paul smiled and said OK. Steve just stared as Paul and I left the bar.

Paul was on me as soon as the car door shut. He said he'd never met anyone like me before. We made out in the front seat for what seemed like a few minutes but was in fact half an hour. Since I lived with my parents and he lived with his girlfriend, we decided to go to a motel.

There were two beds, but one was all we needed. Paul was out of his clothes and in bed before I had a chance to pull my pants down. He told me to hurry up, that he could barely hold on any longer. As I slid between the sheets, he felt my leg on his and turned. He slid his hands over my stomach, then up to my chest; he put one leg on mine, then slid it up and over my crotch. My cock was stone-hard.

Paul's body pressed down on me. This had always been my deepest desire—to be totally possessed by a man, have him on top of me, with my being unable to do anything about it.

I put my palms on his chest and gently pushed up. He pushed back against my hands, and I moaned. He knew it turned me on, so he started being more forceful.

I massaged his back as he lay on top of me and rubbed

his hard cock against mine. My palms worked down toward his ass. "Your hands should be outlawed," Paul said, his eyes right on mine and a smile lighting his face.

I'd never wanted anyone to enter my ass, but now I asked Paul to fuck me. He said, "Can do."

We switched places so I was on top. He lay there with his legs spread and bent, just waiting.

His cock was almost the same size and shape as mine.

As soon as I took him into my mouth, I knew he would not be able to control himself. His back arched, and he let out a loud, ecstatic cry. I was sure he'd wake up the people in the rooms next door. I sucked his cock as if I'd been without one for years, taking all eight inches into my mouth. With his cock deep in my throat, I licked his balls. All I heard was "Oh, God," "Babe," and so on, while my face was locked between his thick, muscular legs.

Suddenly Paul threw me off and onto my back. He held my hands above my head. His eyes had changed; he looked wild, consumed with desire. He gripped both my hands in one of his, then took hold of his cock and put it down by my ass. He asked if this was what I wanted. I didn't move. He put the head of his cock next to my opening. Our sweat and my spit on his cock would be lubricant enough.

Paul spit into his right hand and very slowly moved his grip down my dick. I wanted to come; I had to come. I was about to shoot my load. It was then that I felt his cock enter in one quick thrust. I let out a little moan—it hurt!—but he kept beating me off.

Paul's thrusts were relentless and in perfect rhythm with the hand on my cock. I hooked my legs around his back for comfort and to feel more of his dick inside me. His eyes rolled up in their sockets as he came. I came right after. Paul was breathing hard into my ear.

I could have kept going all night, but instead I drifted off to sleep with that magnificent man still on top of me.

When I woke up the next morning, Paul was studying my face. I smiled. He went to kiss me, and my eager mouth took his tongue. He wasn't drunk any longer, so I guessed he didn't feel any guilt.

Paul pulled back and said that he would love to see me again but that he didn't know what to do about his girlfriend. He wanted me, but past gay relationships had really hurt him. We got up and made plans for the next weekend, Labor Day—my parents would be out of town.

Those seven days went by so slowly, I couldn't believe it. He called me every night. He said that every time he thought about me, he'd get a hard-on. He couldn't have sex with his girlfriend. I felt sorry for her, but I couldn't stop what Paul and I felt for each other.

At last it was Friday evening. Paul arrived just as I pulled in from work. Right there in the front yard, which is screened by trees, he kissed me deeply and hard.

I could barely wait till we went to bed, but first we talked, and I made him dinner. During dessert he took off his shirt, and I dribbled a line of chocolate on his stomach. As I licked it off, Paul laughed and bent over to kiss me. He said he loved me. I looked up and smiled.

S.M., Port Orchard, Wash.

◆ Bells of Glory ◆

Summers in Kentucky are hot and steamy. Still, the work in the fields must go on. I live in a monastery, and we must support ourselves by every means allowed. This summer has been especially hot and dry. With so little rainfall, extra monks were put out in the fields to insure proper irrigation for the crops. Much to my displeasure, I was assigned to help out in the fields, under the direction of Brother Thomas.

Brother Thomas is a man I have been afraid of since I entered the monastery some six years ago. Because of our different job assignments, we have had little contact with each other, and the one time we did, it was disastrous.

I was assigned to clean the rest rooms, and one afternoon I was running around, trying to get them done before I heard the prayer bell. Not realizing that someone was in the bathroom, I opened the door, reached in, and turned off the light. As I did, a voice yelled at me. I immediately went in to see who it was. You guessed it. Brother Thomas.

Even then, he made my knees shake—and not from fear. He was about 6 foot 2 and had the most incredible build I have ever seen on a man. He looked like a football player with a well-sculpted body. The hair on his chest was not too thick and was arranged in a beautiful design. His chest was huge, with well-defined pecs, and his arms were as large as my thighs.

I found myself staring at his beautiful, wet body as he stepped from the shower. Our eyes locked, and he smiled at me. I realized what was happening and made a slight gasping sound and turned to hurry out.

This was the hunk I had been assigned to work under. As soon as I saw him in the field, I could have died. He was wearing jeans and a pair of boots—nothing more. The sun reflected off the sweat already forming on his forehead and hairy chest. Once again found myself staring at his massive pectoral muscles.

Twice during that day Brother Thomas came over to the spot where I was working to check on my progress. The second time he came by to inspect my work, I wasn't wearing my shirt. He looked at me with great delight in his eyes and then ran his hand from the top of his jeans, up across his wet chest to his throat, and then slowly back down to his waist.

Evening finally came, and we all returned to the monastery for a shower. My body ached with pain and from exposure to the sun. After the last prayers were said, the bells for silence rang. I went directly to my room and fell onto my bed, lying there for a few moments without a thought going through my head. It was a quiet night, and the sensation of the sheets against my nude body felt good.

I ran my hand from my throat, down my hairless chest, and across my flat stomach. Then I remembered Brother Thomas doing the same. I reached down and folded my hand around my semihard dick, allowing my little finger to play with the hair on my balls. I realized that I had to piss, so I got up, wrapped a towel around my waist, and went down the hall to the bathroom.

The cool tile felt good against my bare feet. The hall was dark, but I knew my way to the bathroom even in the dark. Unwrapping the towel from around my waist, I stood at the urinal. Just as I was shaking the last drop of piss from my cock, I sensed that I was not alone. I quickly turned my head and saw someone standing in the entrance to one of the shower stalls. It was him.

Standing with his hands over his head, holding on to the upper frame of the door, he was an imposing figure. His chest rose and fell as he breathed. His stomach was flat and well-defined, and his underwear was threadbare, showing his swelling cock. I could see hairs sticking out of the well-worn shorts. My cock began to swell uncontrollably. I was frozen to the spot.

He slowly walked up to me and leaned his face toward mine. I opened my mouth slightly to receive his long, wet tongue.

By the time my hands reached his strong neck, he pulled his tongue out of my mouth and pressed his body against mine. His hands held my ass, one covering each cheek. I could feel his hard dick and the hair on his balls grazing my smooth stomach.

I grabbed his thick neck with both hands. I was going to hold on, no matter what this hunk did to me. He took me into the shower stall and carefully sat me down on the bench just inside the door.

Kneeling in front of me, he kissed me deep and long and then slid his tongue out of my mouth and ran it down over my chin and neck. He continued down my chest and encircled my tit, licking and nibbling it, moving from one to the other. My hard, throbbing cock was now almost between his pecs, and my legs were wrapped around his body.

As he moved to my stomach, I knew I would explode the minute he wrapped his lips around my shaft. I did not want to come yet, but there was no stopping this man. He was in control, and I was going to let him do his thing.

Slowly he began to lick and suck my nuts, first one and then the other. Next he ran his tongue under my nuts, toward my asshole. I didn't know if I was going to live to tell about it; the sensation was almost more than I could take.

Taking both my nuts into his mouth again, he rubbed his nose alongside my stiff cock. He breathed through his nose, and the rush of air sent chills all over my body. Then he released my balls and ran his tongue up the underside of my cock. My dick jumped several times before he reached the head. Taking my nuts in one hand, he squeezed and pulled them while he pushed my eight-inch cock all the way down his throat in one smooth motion.

He moved his lips around the base and blew the air out

his nose and into my pubic hair. He clamped his mouth around the base of my cock and pulled up with his neck, almost lifting me off the bench. His grip was keeping the come from shooting out my cock.

He had pulled the skin up with his mouth so that my cock head was covered with my foreskin, and then he licked the head of my cock. Still holding my nuts, he let the foreskin go by releasing his lips, and it pulled back down from the head and his tongue. He licked the head very slowly. At that point his grip was not going to be able to hold back the rush of come.

With his lips locked around the base of my cock, the stream of hot come began to rush up my shaft and into his throat.

T.W., Tucson, Ariz.

◆ Boys' Night Out ◆

The man of my fantasies is my best friend's husband. Claire and I grew up together. We were inseparable in grade school, even dated in junior high. She was the first person I told that I was gay, which made us grow even closer. In college she met and married Rodney.

Back then all three of us were overweight and out of shape. So we decided to work out together. After a few weeks Claire lost interest, but Rodney and I continued. He worked harder than I did. I tried to keep up. Watching him exercise and build his muscles all those months made me proud of who he had become: a lean, muscular hunk instead of a cute, chubby guy. I loved watching him work out, flexing, sweating, grunting, and groaning. He liked having me around to spot him. Even in the shower he was always horsing around, cracking jokes, poking fun at us for trying to become hunks. His body was shaping up nicely, more so than mine. He had a flat stomach, bulging thighs, strong arms, and a great pair of pecs.

I had great wet dreams about him plowing my butt with his hard cock, pushing it deeper, faster in my gut, then coming all over me. Some nights I could feel his cock in my mouth. It was big, thick, and firm, with a taste of musk. When I woke up I was all damp and sticky. I loved Claire, but I lusted after Rodney. I knew it was wrong, but I didn't want to stop it.

One night when Claire was out of town, we went barhopping. Rodney called it "boys' night out." He knew I was gay and insisted on going to some of "my places." It was great. I loved having an attractive man on my arm. A bartender asked us if we were lovers. Rodney laughed and said, "Yes." My heart swelled, my head spun. I was light-headed all evening. We drank too much and ended up at my place, of course.

We entered laughing and giggling like schoolboys and fell onto the couch. Rodney cuddled into my arms and passed out. I was so nervous, I couldn't sleep. I was afraid he would wake up and see my erection and hate me. But as the night passed, he would wake up and remove some clothes. First his shirt went, then his shoes. I fell asleep at one point only to be awakened by Rodney taking his pants off. Then he said, "Let's go to bed."

He grabbed my hand and walked me to my bed. He crawled under the covers. I stripped quickly and climbed in with him. We cuddled together and fell asleep. We slept that way all night. In the morning when we woke up, he kissed me good morning and acted like it was natural for us to wake up nude with hard-ons. I kissed him hard and long.

Then he rolled on top of me, grinding his cock into mine. Slowly he went down on me, taking my cock into his mouth. He worked it gently. He was so persuasive and sensual that I shot all over his face.

Then I did him, sucked him like it was the last cock I was ever going to have. I was frantic, trying to take all he had and more. I wouldn't let him free. I sucked him dry.

After he came, he was still friendly, making jokes and touching me. We showered and dressed. I fed him breakfast, and then he left. We even made plans to work out that afternoon, which we did.

We see each other all the time. I haven't said anything to Claire. Neither has Rodney. We haven't talked about it, but in the shower he keeps grabbing my butt. I know he wants it again, but I'm waiting for him to make the first move. I hope he hurries because I am ready to burst!

D.T., San Antonio, Tex.

◆ By Far the Best Man ◆

I never thought I'd be writing to your magazine, and maybe what I have to say won't even qualify. You see, I'm basically straight. I have a brand-new wife, and we want kids and a house—the whole nine yards. But what happened to me at my bachelor party really was a fantasy, though I never would have admitted it before.

My best friend, Tony, set up this outrageous bachelor party for me as soon as he heard that Jill and I were going to get married. He hired strippers, got fuck films—the whole bit. He wanted me to go out in a blaze of glory.

So on the night of the party, all these guys started showing up, and the party got rolling pretty quickly.

The films were hot, the girls were hot, and everything was about to explode. But for some reason it really wasn't getting to me. I don't know why, but the films and the chicks just weren't affecting me the way they should; they weren't stiffening my rod.

I shrugged it off as cold feet and headed for the john to get rid of some of the beer I had been guzzling. I knew in my heart that in 24 hours I'd be attempting to prove my manhood to Jill.

Just as I was shaking the last drops of piss from my dick, the head door opened, and Brian walked in. He was a good buddy; I worked with him at the branch downtown. I knew he was gay, and I could tell from his eyes that he was being as tolerant as he could.

"Must be a drag for you, huh, Brian?" I said as I zipped up my fly.

"Oh, let's say I'm chalking it up as an educational experience." He winked. "I gotta say this: It beats PBS."

We both laughed and talked some more. After a few minutes he noticed that I seemed to be miles away. He seemed genuinely concerned, so I told him about my doubts about Jill and all. I know he sensed it was something deeper, so I seized the opportunity and broached the subject of homosexuality.

He was very patient with me, and he answered all my questions. I told him I was sure I wasn't gay but that I had some nagging curiosities.

He handled them all. And he handled me too—rather well, I'd say. The next hour was one of the best in my life.

We stole out of the hall, where the party was going at full steam, and took cover in his car, an old BMW with a huge backseat.

He started very slowly with me, stroking my hair and my

face, talking to me. The thing that really worked with Brian was that I considered us great friends. I know that with anyone else it would have seemed ludicrous.

He guided me through my initiation with a deftness and sensitivity I'd never received from a lover before. And I was glad my first taste of cock came from him. It was delicious. The whole time I sucked on his whang, I knew in the back of my head that this couldn't be a one-night affair, that I'd be back for more.

And when he took my throbbing piece between his lips, I thought I'd die. Nobody had ever sucked me off like that before, and I resigned myself to thinking that nobody ever would again—at least, nobody but Brian.

He brought me off to an incredible climax. My wad shot at least two feet in front of me. And my screams were wild and primitive, full of pure lust and genuine love.

I will never consider what I did that night wrong, and I'll never entirely divulge exactly all that we did. It was very special to me. It was pure sex and pure love, mixed for the first time in my life.

I went ahead and married Jill the next day—more out of cowardice than love—but I refuse to give up my feelings for Brian. I know in my heart that things will change eventually. And if not, I'll always have a send-off like nobody's ever gotten before.

P.W., Maywood, Ill.

◆ Christmas ◆

Charlie strides along the trail, about 30 yards ahead of me. His long legs carry him along effortlessly, just as they have for the last ten miles, out and back on the Rocky Mountain Trail. He still has the energy to hop over the dead branches and boulders that block the trail. Fucker!

Charlie is a very well-put-together guy. He rowed on the crew in prep school and in college and has the broadest, thickest shoulders I've ever seen. He isn't great-looking, but what he lacks in looks he makes up for with his sensational body and his charm. I can see why he never has any trouble with the girls. He isn't wearing a shirt, just chinos and hiking boots. Charlie never wears jeans, just washed-out unironed chinos. The thin cotton of his chinos drapes sensuously over his butt. He wears his pants so low, I can see the blue band of his boxer shorts.

If I were closer, I could probably see the patch of curly blond fur at the base of his spine. I've been following Charlie around for a long time. I know this kind of thing. Charlie and I have been skinny-dipping and taking showers together for years, and some things you can't help noticing. Charlie has big balls and the loosest, lowest-hanging scrotum I've ever seen. I'm always amazed that he can hike in those shorts.

I find a convenient slab of granite and sit down, exhausted and thirsty. I'm tired of eating Charlie's dust. It takes only a minute or two for him to sense that I've stopped. Charlie's like that. He has an incredible sense of place—of *his* place—and what's around him. I watch as he turns around, then look down at the dusty gravel as he heads back up the trail toward me.

"What's the matter? Tired?" Charlie is smiling, but I can tell by the furrows on his brow that he's annoyed. He had been in his own world, eating up the trail, thinking whatever he thinks in the long silences that punctuate my experience with him.

He sits down next to me and hands me his canteen. His shoulder brushes against mine. I take the canteen. I'm thirsty. The warmth radiating from his body feels good in the cold air, but I slide away an inch. I can't take the touch of his flesh on mine. I look back at the ground, but what I see are Charlie's long legs, stretched out across the trail.

"You OK?" he asks.

I grimace and, without looking up, mutter, "I'm fine, just fine. Just go on ahead. It's not far to the trail head. I'll meet you back at the van."

Charlie's VW van, fitted out as a camper, is parked on a turnout, about a mile down the road from where the trail meets the two-lane mountain road.

Charlie shrugs, apparently indifferent. "Suit yourself. See you later." In a couple of minutes he has disappeared around the side of the hill. All I hear is the sound of the wind in the trees and his receding footsteps.

This has been a bad day. Charlie and I are best friends. We know each other too well. And it's been a long summer. Something has gotten to me, I don't know what it is—maybe just too much time on the road, three weeks that we've been exploring the Rockies, driving from trail head to trail head.

I get up. My legs ache. The blisters from my too-heavy, too-new boots don't feel any better for the few minutes' rest. But as I start off down the trail, at least I'm not staring at fucking Charlie's fucking back! I'm in a terrible mood. I'm still thirsty. My head aches from the altitude.

And then there's Charlie.

Charlie and I had spent that summer at a farmstead in the rolling green farm county of Wisconsin, the ramshackle house a refuge for an ever-changing tribe of college drop-outs and perpetual graduate students. Charlie, who was the former, and I, who was the latter, were inseparable. We shared our money and whatever drugs came our way. When one of us was between girlfriends, the other would play consoler and matchmaker.

Almost every night we would walk together up the steep hill behind the farmhouse, through the hickory grove at the top of the hill, past the pond, and along the ridge to a bluff that faced the distant gleaming curve of the Wisconsin River. Charlie's long legs are up the hillside behind the house, and I was always a few yards behind him. That's when I became familiar with Charlie's unique graceful, loping stride, which I tried my best to imitate. In between taking in the view and the starry sky, I would take in the vision of Charlie's back. He had just finished his senior year on the varsity crew, and Charlie was in his prime.

When we got to the bluff, we'd lie on the grass for hours, side by side, looking out at the river or up at the stars. And we'd talk. He was reading Toynbee. I was working my way through *War and Peace*. We'd talk about history, music, girl trouble…

Our end-of-summer trip out West had been great, at least up until the last couple of days. For some reason he had stopped talking. And today had been the worst. Charlie's charm had turned to civility, and I had grown increasingly resentful. I couldn't figure it out. Maybe it was too much Charlie. Maybe it was time for a break.

When I finally get to the highway, the sun has set behind the broken ridgeline of the Rockies, but twilight lingers on. Although the sky is fairly bright, the thin air is losing heat fast now that the sun is blocked by the enormous wall of mountains.

By the time I limp the downhill mile to where the camper is parked, it's nearly dark. There's no light coming from the windows of the VW. That means Charlie, with all the energy in the world, has walked or hitchhiked the two miles down the road into Estes Park. Right now he's sitting at a bar having a beer and a burger, and, if I know Charlie, he's chatting up a couple of pretty townies. The bastard will probably get laid before the night is through.

And I'm stuck up here in the cold on this godforsaken hill, with nothing to eat but what's in the cooler. I fumble at the lock of the sliding side door. A car goes by, laboring its way up the hill. Its headlights glare on the side of the van. My key slips into the lock. The car's taillights disappear around the bend in the road, leaving behind darkness even deeper than before.

I'm a city boy, and I never feel quite safe in the eerie quiet of a country night. I shudder and scramble into the van and slide the door shut behind me. The camper is set up in two sections. The kitchen is in front, just behind the driver's and passenger's seats. It has a built-in bench, sink, propane stove, cooler, and Formica counter grubby with crumbs and dried-out smears of jam. Charlie isn't a model of neatness, and I've given up cleaning up after him. In the rear there's a platform covered by a foam pad, just wide enough for our two sleeping bags.

I sit on the bench for a minute or two, forlornly staring out the window at the dark mass of trees silhouetted against the evening sky. After a while, feeling safe here in the familiar enclosure of the camper, I slide the door open.

I pull off my boots and socks and rub my aching feet, then rummage in the cooler for whatever scraps there are to eat. A couple of apples, just on the edge of shriveling; a hunk of cheese, not bad once I scrape off the mold; and half a box of saltines. I won't starve. And there's plenty of water.

When I finish eating, I jump out onto the gravel and strip off my jeans, Jockey shorts, and T-shirt. I wipe myself down with a cold wet cloth. It isn't a hot shower, but it feels good just to wipe off the dust and the sweat. I pull my shorts back on and slide into my down bag, shivering as the cold nylon hits my bare flesh. I close my eyes and try not to think about Charlie, in town with hot food and a cold beer, charming the locals.

I wake up in a sweat. It's cold outside, but the sleeping bag is too warm, and the camper really holds the heat. I unzip my bag and throw it open and lie there for a moment, sweating. I shove open the rear door of the van and step out into the cold. I'm naked except for my shorts, but the cold air feels good on my bare skin. I limp over to the edge of the gravel shoulder, pull down my shorts, and piss down the side of the hill. There's a stream running down there in the dark. I can hear the water rushing over the rocks. My own stream just goes on and on, steaming in the cold. This actually feels good.

I look up at the sky. And there, standing out among the magnificent blanket of stars, is Orion, the hunter. Below his belt, defining the mighty hunter's thigh, is Rigel, one of the brightest of the stars. A Christmas star. Christmas, three months and 1,500 miles away. Why do I think of Christmas now? Because it's cold and dark? Because there's a bright star? I decide it doesn't have to make sense.

For the first time in days, I escape a cloud of gloom and smile. I shake the last drops of piss off my cock and stuff it back into my shorts. A sudden breeze comes up the hillside. I might be happy, but I'm practically naked, and it's cold. I look up at Orion one last time, then climb back into the van and lie down on my open sleeping bag.

I fall into a deep sleep, so I'm not sure how much time goes by. I hear a car, only the second I've heard all night. The car's headlights destroy the night, and I'm back in the evil place I've been in all day. Every sound carries in the crystal-clear silence of the night. The car pulls to a halt across the road. The door opens, and I hear Charlie's voice, husky and maybe a little bit slurred with beer, say "Thanks for the lift."

The car door slams shut. I hear Charlie's boots first on the asphalt, then on the gravel shoulder. Charlie stands at the side of the road, right outside the VW. I hear him piss, an amazingly loud, long stream. He must have had more than a couple of beers. But Charlie can handle it.

Charlie opens the sliding door. As he steps in, the right side of the van settles down on its springs. Charlie is a big man. He sits on the bench in the kitchen area, just inches from my head, and takes off his boots and socks. Charlie is humming a little tune, softly, so as not to wake me up. "Rat-a-tat-tat-tat!" "The Little Drummer Boy?" It can't be. I must be dreaming.

I am lying on my side, my back to Charlie's side of the foam pad. I keep my breathing deep and even, in what I hope is a convincing simulation of deep sleep. I hear a rustle of clothes as Charlie strips off his T-shirt, then his chinos. He's down to his boxer shorts. Even though I have my back to him, even though my eyes are closed tight, I know. Charlie always sleeps in his boxers. He packed half a dozen pairs, each of faded almost-worn-out blue broadcloth.

Charlie climbs onto the pad and kneels near my head. He's so close that I feel the wave of heat that radiates from his body. He unzips his bag and lies down. But he doesn't settle in. He doesn't zip up his bag. He must be lying there on his back, looking up at the roof of the camper. Naked, like me, except for his shorts. He folds his hands behind his head. I can tell because I smell sweat. Neither of us has been near a shower for a couple of days, but Charlie's sweat smells good—clean and athletic.

Without thinking about it, I breathe in a little deeper, taking in Charlie's smell. I feel a surge in my crotch. I don't know what that's about, and I get scared and pull my bag even farther up around my head. But the down holds the heat, and the nylon sticks to my body. I start to sweat. You don't want to start sweating inside a down bag.

Charlie doesn't move. He lies on his back for a few more minutes, but I can tell from his breathing that he isn't settling into sleep. He rolls over onto his right side. The camper is narrow, and Charlie's face is only a few inches from the back of my head.

"Will," he whispers. "Will."

There's a kind of nervous hoarseness in his voice. Charlie is never nervous.

"Huh?" I mumble, still pretending to be asleep. I roll over onto my back. The sleeping bag slips open over my chest. I'm trembling. I look down at myself. My chest shines with sweat. I start to shiver. What has gotten into me? I don't have a clue.

"Will," Charlie whispers, "I was thinking..." He pauses.

I don't answer. I just lie there sweating and shivering. Charlie's face is only a few inches from my ear. His body smells of a day's worth of sweat, his breath of beer and cigarettes. Why do I think he smells great? I feel cold and hot at the same time. I'm not mad anymore, just scared. I don't know what's going on, or maybe I do. Either way, I'm scared. Instead of answering, I swallow and lie there, looking up at the roof of the van.

Finally, an aeon later, I get up enough courage to glance over at Charlie. There's not much light, and his hair falls down over his face, but I can see his dark brown eyes. He's looking down at me. I look back up at the roof.

I haven't answered, but Charlie doesn't give up. He's had a couple of beers, and whatever it is he wants, he's out to get it. "Will, I was thinking, what if we just took off our clothes and sort of, uh…sort of rolled around together?" He pauses and takes a long, deep breath. "You know, just kind of wrestled…" He swallows and lies there, his head propped on his elbow, looking down at me.

I lie there, frozen. We've wrestled before, just horsing around. Charlie must have 30 pounds on me, so it's never much of a match. If we're going to wrestle, why do we have to take our clothes off? Besides, I think with terrible lucidity, we have almost no clothes to take off.

I squeeze my eyes shut and lie frozen, scared to death. What the fuck is happening? I'm sweating. I'm shivering like crazy. I feel my balls tighten up into my crotch. The word *no* forms somewhere in the back of my throat and works its way up toward my lips. But the word won't come out. It's right there, on the tip of my tongue, "No." This just isn't right. What the fuck is Charlie thinking? Guys just don't do things like that.

"No." I have formed the word. But my lips are clamped

shut. One very simple word. I force my mouth open, ready to say "No."

But I don't.

My mind is racing a million miles a minute. I can't imagine where this is headed. But somehow I know it's not about rolling around and wrestling with a buddy who's had a couple of beers. Never once in my life did I ever know I wanted this, whatever it is. I'm not a *faggot.* I'm not a *fairy.* I'm not *queer.* I have a girlfriend. Charlie and I both have great sex with our girlfriends. We talk about it all the time.

One very simple word, "No." All ready to go.

But the word won't come out. Through the cloud of fear and confusion, the bright star of what I really want starts to shine through. The part of me that has always known is fighting with the part of me that doesn't want to know. "This is what you've always wanted." "No." "This is what you've waited for ever since Charlie first stuck his head in the door of your dorm room." "No!" "This is something you've waited for all your life." *"No!"*

I'm a sweating, shivering bundle of misery. Somehow I force my lips open and a word comes out. "OK." Charlie doesn't say anything. I listen as he pulls his boxers down over his ankles. He isn't kidding. I look over to his side of the pad. He's lying on his back, staring up at the roof. Charlie is naked. His crotch is hidden in shadow.

This is for real. It's my turn. I hook my thumbs under the elastic of my shorts and pull down. My shorts get hung up around my ankles, but I kick them off. I'm scared to death. Maybe we both are, because Charlie doesn't move either. We both just lie there. Naked.

We hear a car, its motor laboring up the hill, the first car in an hour. The park ranger? We lie there, frozen. I glance over at Charlie. He is absolutely motionless. He's holding his breath. So am I. The glare of the headlights shines through the translucence of the fogged-up windows. We've got the van so heated up, the windows are dripping with dew. No one can see us. The car drives by. The sound of the motor fades into the distance.

It's dark again, and at last it happens. Charlie throws a hairy leg over my legs. His arm is around my shoulder. And he's on top of me. He's a big man. There's no way I'm going to move. His two-day beard grinds into my neck. Charlie puts his weight on his elbows, and I push up off my back and slide out from under him. He sort of kneels there, a little bit of air between his belly and the pad. I wrap my arm around his waist and pull him toward me. We wrestle. I'm in heaven.

Charlie is nearly a head taller than I am. But somehow we fit. We roll around on the pad for a while, shoving, pulling, twisting. At one point Charlie pins me on my belly, and I feel his big balls flop down on the small of my back. We lie on our sides, panting for breath, belly to belly. He places his big feet under mine and presses up on the balls of my feet. I feel his chest heaving up against mine.

And I feel something else. A miracle. Charlie's cock. Charlie has a big cock, but I've seen it only soft. It is pressed against my body, and I feel it thickening and growing. It feels big! I get scared, but there's no stopping now. I slide my hand along his hip and down toward his crotch. My fingers comb through the tangled bush at the base of his belly. The back of my hand grazes the side of his cock. He's hard. Really hard. So am I.

We're not wrestling anymore. We don't even pretend to wrestle. Charlie and I are making love. We don't kiss—for some reason we're not ready for that—but we are definitely making love. Charlie is all lean muscle on a big-boned frame. Perfect, smooth skin with silky hair on his chest and belly and arms and legs. And a healthy, sweaty animal smell. I nestle my head into Charlie's armpit and breathe deep. I drive in, grazing in the tangle of hair, sucking up the juicy sweat. Our cocks rub against each other stroking, probing.

I get brave and reach down between Charlie's legs. I wrap my hand around his cock, stroke it all the way down to the root, buried in its nest of pubic hair.

Charlie yanks himself away. "Hey!" he shouts. He sounds mad. His voice reverberates off glass and metal. Charlie slams me back against the side of the van. He jumps on top of me and lays his forearm across my throat, cutting off the air. He looks down at me in apparent fury. "Keep your fucking hands to yourself," he says. But Charlie is only playing, because the next thing he does is to lean down and stick his tongue in my ear. He slips his free hand between us and down to my crotch. I feel his calluses as he wraps his hand around my cock and strokes it. Heaven.

We're new at this, but we know what we want. We've done it with women, and we know what to do. Maybe real men don't kiss. Maybe real men don't suck cock. But there's something real men do. They *fuck!*

Charlie pushes me onto my back and slips his hand between my thighs. Two men wrestling in an enclosed space generate a lot of heat. It's hot and damp, and we're sweating like pigs. I have my legs clenched tight, but my thighs are so wet, his hands slips through, right to the spot he's looking for.

We are totally naive about this. Virgins. There isn't a drop of lube within reaching distance. But there's sweat. And spit. And a lifetime of waiting. I rock my hips up and wrap my legs around Charlie's waist. Charlie presses up against me. He's slick with sweat and spit. But he's big. I don't have anything to compare it with, but right then I figure that he's *really* big. I do my best to open up, but he's pressing up against a door that's never been opened, not from that direction.

It hurts. It really hurts. But I want him so bad, I don't care. Charlie wants to get inside of me, and that's all that matters. Once he's in, he lays into me with all his weight, and for the first time in my life I feel the magnificent long stroke of a man's cock in my ass. This is a virgin fuck, so it doesn't take long. Charlie arches his back and looks up at the ceiling, and I'm looking up at this man's body, a perfect arc of lean, straining muscles, all focused on dropping his load deep in my ass. I come at the same time Charlie does, no hands.

Christmas.

Charlie's body sags down on top of mine. He rests his head on my shoulder. He's so heavy, I have trouble breathing. I don't care. What matters is that I have Charlie's come inside me. His big hairy, muscular body, a *man's body,* covers me. I wrap my arms around his waist. I feel safe.

After a while Charlie wriggles his hips and smears the mess on our bellies around in our tangled belly hair. We laugh. Charlie pulls out, rolls off me, and reaches for his shorts. I grab his wrist. I don't want this to end.

"Don't get dressed," I say. "Let's stay naked."

"It's OK," he says. His voice is whispery soft, husky from sex. "Just relax."

He uses the shorts to wipe off my belly, then wipes himself off. He lies on his back. I pull myself up against him and throw my leg across his thighs and hold him tight. We lie there, content, amazed, silent. I don't have anything to say. What do you say to your straight-jock best friend who's just given you your first fuck?

I'm getting hard again, and I don't know what to do about it. Charlie does. He grips my ass with his hand and pulls me toward him, pressing my cock against his side. Charlie twists away from me and rolls over onto his side of the pad. He sprawls out belly-down, arms over his head. Charlie is two-toned, tanned from the waist up and pure white below. His ass gleams pearly white in the starlight. He looks over at me and raises his eyebrows and beckons me with his head. He whimpers. He flexes his ass. He rotates and lifts his hips. He spreads his legs.

I get the idea.

I climb on top of him and kneel between his legs. I can't believe what I see. The powerful V of Charlie's back; his narrow waist; the tuft of sun-bleached hair above his ass crack; the dark, secret crevice between the mounds of white… My mouth is dry as sand, but Charlie reaches back with a handful of spit. I reach in, and there it is, nestled in the sweat-matted curly hairs that cloak his ass. Christmas!

Hours later we've worn each other out. Charlie is sound asleep. I stumble outside to pee, the air bitter cold against my naked flesh. I look up in the sky, but Orion has already set—the magnificent hunter gone home from the hunt.

This isn't the beginning of a honeymoon. Charlie and I will have our troubles. But when summer comes again and I follow Charlie up the hill behind the house, through the hickory grove, past the pond, and out onto the bluff, there'll be more for us there than conversation with a best friend. There'll be a summer, maybe two, of lying naked together under the stars, making love, having it now, all of it, not waiting for Christmas.

J.S., Los Angeles, Calif.

◆ Connubial Bliss ◆

On the Saturday before last Valentine's Day, my kid brother married his college sweetheart. I was to be his best man. It was during the rehearsal at the church that I first met Jean-Marc, the husband of the bride's younger sister. He was also in the wedding party. His wife, who was more than eight months' pregnant, understandably chose not to be her sister's matron of honor.

Jean-Marc was of French-Canadian descent and spoke with a very heavy accent. He was the most breathtaking young man I've ever seen! He was 24, stood about 6 foot 4, and was built like a bodybuilder. He had sexy violet-blue eyes, light sandy blond hair, and a boyishly handsome face that dimpled with his killer smile. He reminded me of a young Jean-Claude Van Damme—not because of the way he looked but because of his mannerisms and accent. I later found out he was a personal trainer by profession. I could not take my eyes off him, but knowing he was off-limits, I controlled my urge to stare at him that whole night.

At the wedding reception the next night, I couldn't help watching him as he danced with his wife. It was only too obvious from the bulge in the crotch of his snug-fitting tuxedo pants that he was hung like a proverbial horse. I grew fascinated with his oversize basket—I was dying to see what he had! I fantasized about what it would look like. My dick was aching with lust.

I saw him leave the ballroom to go to the rest room. Ignoring my conscience, I followed him. When I entered the washroom, he was already standing at the urinal pissing. I went to the urinal next to his, withdrew my swelling cock, and proceeded to empty my own bladder. Nonchalantly I stole a glance at his flaccid ten-inch cock and his large, hairy balls. His genitals were more beautiful than I could have imagined. My own cock grew hard in my hand. "Hi, Jean-Marc," I said hoarsely, eyeing his magnificent cock as he urinated.

"Hi," he replied as he slowly pulled the wrinkly foreskin back along the thick shaft of his swelling cock and revealed the fat, plumlike head. "Like what you see?"

"What?" I said nervously. I was caught red-handed. I could feel my face flush with embarrassment.

"Your brother told us you are gay," he continued, "but I didn't believe him because you don't look like a fag. That is, not till I noticed you staring at me all night. You're hot for my dick, aren't you?"

I threw caution to the wind. "Fuck, yes," I replied.

"I heard fags are great cocksuckers," he remarked, then flashed that killer smile. "Are you any good?"

"Are you asking me to suck your cock?" I said.

"I'm not queer," he retorted stiffly, but then he relaxed, and a smirk flashed across his handsome face. "But as you can see, my wife's due to drop at any minute, and sex with her is out of the question right now."

"So let me guess," I replied. "You're horny and want a quick blow job to tide you over."

He smiled. "Why not?"

I was so excited that my knees quivered with anticipation. I gave him my hotel-room number and left the men's room. Minutes later he knocked on my door. I let him in and locked the door as he quickly unzipped his fly and pulled out his huge cock. Eagerly I dropped to my knees and took the tip in my mouth, tonguing and sucking it.

"Oh, yeah, you *are* good," he grunted as he began to fuck my face. He humped like a wild man; it was as if he hadn't had sex in months (which certainly could have been the case)! I undid the clasp of his pants and yanked them down his muscular legs. Then I cupped his buttocks and pulled him against me, swallowing even more of his throbbing cock. His balls slapped against my chin.

I wanted more, and I sensed he did too. I pulled my head back and withdrew his pulsing cock from my mouth. "Fuck my ass," I demanded. Without waiting for an answer, I stood and began to undress. Soon we were both nude and on the bed, with his giant cock up my ass. It was one of the best fucks I've ever had! As he pounded my ass, I jacked off and came all over the bedspread.

Afterward we dressed and returned to the reception. I haven't seen him since, but my brother told me that Jean-Marc's wife had a baby boy shortly afterward!

K.J., Dearborn, Mich.

◆ Deep South ◆

His name was Chip. Not that it matters now to anyone but me—and maybe to him, wherever he is. After all, 26 years is a long time. I'm likely the only one who remembers these events because I'm the one to whom these events meant the most.

Chip was an active in our fraternity hierarchy; I was a lowly pledge. Even so, I was older than he was (our urban university's student body represented an amazingly diverse mix of backgrounds and ages—much more so than you might find at your typical Southern college).

Our chapter house was just that: a house, an old Victorian mansion that the university owned and allowed our fraternity to use. A few of the brothers actually lived on the premises, but for the most part the upstairs bedrooms and beds were considered communal property and available to any of the members on a "first come, first served" basis depending on who had a hot date and, just as likely, who had to sleep off overindulgence in booze. On major party weekends it was not uncommon or unusual for two tanked-up, passed-out guys to share the same bed.

I don't remember how Chip and I began to hit it off so well. Unlike me, he was not much on participating in campus activities. He was only an average student at best, and our backgrounds were vastly different. Further, he didn't take a great deal of interest in the fraternity itself, while I, as a pledge, had to take such interest.

Still, there must have been some kind of attraction there because after I pledged we quickly became as close and as inseparable as a pledge and an active were allowed to be. (I was given lots of leeway because, even though I was a pledge, I was 21 and one of only two members old enough to buy beer and liquor for the other guys!)

My growing up had been somewhat sheltered, while Chip's was anything but sheltered. And after all, one of the unspoken promises of higher education was that it would bring different kinds of people together. I helped Chip with his assignments; he taught me how to ride a motorcycle. He learned a little about theater and music from me; I gained some useful street smarts from him. There was a good and comfortable mutuality about us.

One cold weekend in the late fall, a major house party was breaking up when I was called from work duties to the phone. Chip, who had left earlier, was calling me from the city jail. He had been arrested for drunk driving and begged me to come get him out.

For some reason the thought of Chip's being locked in a cell with God knows who disturbed me. A lot. I immediately left the house and went to find a bonding company to spring him. Within an hour that task was accomplished.

Chip's car had been impounded, so I drove him back to the frat house.

All the other members were now either passed out or gone, so we had the downstairs completely to ourselves. We were both kind of stressed out, so we shared a few drinks, to the point that we could finally laugh about what had happened to him—and about what *might* have happened to him in that jail cell! In fact, Chip had gotten himself pretty much drunk again and had even reached that point of expressing the "special love" that one drunk feels for another as he repeatedly hugged me, grateful for getting him out of the hoosegow. I finally suggested that we go upstairs and try to find a bedroom or at least a bed. At this point Chip was glad to oblige.

The only space available was what most of the brothers would have called the least desirable room: very small and narrow with only one single bed.

But we cheerfully accepted it as our lot. And, yes, I actually looked forward to sharing a bed with Chip as I had just recently begun to admit to myself that I had a huge crush on him.

OK, I've read these kinds of stories before, and some of the guys who relate these tales say they feel a bit frightened and tentative when finding themselves in my situation. Hell! I wasn't the least bit scared. On the contrary, I was excited and horny and hoping that Chip was feeling the same way. I think my attraction to other guys had only lately begun to pointedly exert itself. Up until that cold November night, I really hadn't been able to explore it in any way other than imaginings, masturbation, and the sensual surprise of the occasional wet dream.

So I quietly gloated about the fact that even if nothing of what I fantasized came of this night, I would at least be spending the next six or eight hours close to and almost naked with my favorite frat brother.

We both stripped down to our underpants; white Jockeys for me, trim white boxers for Chip. For the first time since I'd known him, I was able to look closely at his nearly nude body. Five feet, ten inches tall, he had smooth, nearly hairless skin and a slender, swimmer's build that seemed to silently beg for cuddling. He had long, curly dirty blond hair. God! It was hair to run one's fingertips through. His facial features were both well-defined and well-balanced, and he had moderately thick, sensuous lips. In his inebriated state, he stumbled up against me a few times as we crawled into the barrow bed. His body was warm, and the chill of the night really necessitated our snuggling up to one another.

"You don't mind do you?" was my rhetorical question as I spooned Chip's backside and draped my right arm over his torso.

"No, man. It's fine." Then—wonder of wonders—he grabbed my right hand and held onto it hard as he seemed to drift off to sleep. All of this preliminary touch-feely stuff was just what I had dreamed of! As my lips came to rest on his bare shoulder, my dick was pointing upward toward the restraining waistband of my Jockeys and, at the same time, pressing hard through thin layers of cotton into the perfectly fitted crevice of Chip's butt. My cock began throbbing with passionate jolts of the body electric. As it did so, his grip on my hand conversely relaxed a bit as he began snoring gently. Then, as I succeeded in pulling him even closer and tighter, he stirred for just a moment and then began snoring again as he turned over completely. My beautiful Chip was now facing me. His lips were so close on my pillow that I could see them gently vibrate with every cycle of his breathing.

Slowly—I don't think anything could have stopped me—I began pulling my right leg, jackknifelike, upward toward our almost entwined bodies so that my right knee was headed slowly but directly toward his crotch. After all, I knew damn well what was going on with my dick! I just had to find out if the same thing was happening to his!

Slowly, gently my knee edged forward across my other leg. Jesus! Chip chose that exact moment to pull himself still closer to me. I looked at him in the filtered moonlight, and I swear there was this welcoming smile on his face as he drew closer. I held my breath. Suddenly skin met skin! In its hardness, his cock must have poked through the fly of his shorts, and it was now stiffly pressed against my knee. I didn't take my eyes off Chip's face and sleepy smile as my hand gave in to a sudden, seductive desire to explore what my bare knee had discovered down there.

I'd had no experience doing this kind of thing, but somehow—powerful instincts, I guess—I just knew to grab hold of him in much the same way I liked to hold myself when jacking off. After all, there was that chemistry between the two of us. It had to mean something, didn't it?

In all those past months I had never seen Chip's dick, but as I held it I knew it was perfect for him—and for me. He and I were about the same size: neither of us huge, maybe about six or seven inches hard. A nice fit.

Oh, my God! I thought. *I've actually got a guy's—no, Chip's—dick in my hand, and it feels great!* His short hairs had me by the fingers, and I wasn't about to let go! And, even better than that, he was oozing just a tad—a gentle offertory of the world's most natural lubricant.

I rubbed my thumb in it for a second. He jerked wonderfully in response, and then I began to masturbate him.

As I did, I wondered if he would respond or if he would just remain asleep. There was still that smile on his face, but he was really a mystery to me just then.

I sensed that he might be close to climax. "What if…?" I whispered. Could he hear me? I searched his benign face for a clue, then slithered gently down under the covers. I paused only when I could easily take his pulsing dick between my lips. In less than a minute, ecstasy overtook him as he filled my mouth with his jism, eruption after fiery eruption. Even under the covers I could hear him moan as he brought his hands to the top of my head and began playing with my hair.

I moved back up in the bed. He was still smiling—perhaps more broadly than before—but now his eyes were open and staring into mine. He mouthed the words "I love you" as his fingers fumbled with the waistband of my briefs and the virgin manhood barely contained there.

In the South at that time, 1971, our situation called for the utmost discretion.

But we weren't discreet enough. On a Saturday night a couple of months later, we were caught flagrante delicto (i.e., "dick in mouth") by the two most bigoted rednecks in the chapter. We were given no choice but to depledge and resign.

That's probably when my idealized relationship began to unravel. The fraternity meant almost nothing to Chip. On the other hand, it meant a great deal to me. I don't want to psychoanalyze myself too much, but I suspect that up until Chip and I made love, I had halfway sublimated my homosexual desires into some sort of vital need for the all-male camaraderie, closeness, and intimacy offered by the Greek system. Those feelings for the group didn't disappear immediately just because I'd found a meaningful relationship. The original Greeks, as gay and literate as they were, must have had a word for all of this!

After severing my connection with the group, I became somewhat depressed. My situation was aggravated when Chip began to entertain "other interests"—namely, girls. Once, while on a subsequent trip to Florida for the purpose of recapturing our early magic, I woke up one night to find him in the middle of having sex with a high school girl whose folks were staying in the same motel! He and I soon went our separate ways after reaching the mutual conclusion that he was primarily heterosexual.

You know, I still have our composite fraternity photograph on the wall in my kitchen, and I don't think a week has gone by during the last quarter century that I haven't thought about him and looked at his picture at least once. Some "connections"—even seemingly "one way" connections—are so vital to our being that even 25 years of silence cannot sunder them. In that long-unrequited, odd sort of way, I still feel a lot of love for Chip.

P.C., Birmingham, Ala.

◆ Doctor's Orders ◆

My name is Trey. I work with my dad on a horse ranch in northern Texas. The ranch has been in the family for years. My dad started me out just feeding the horses and cleaning the stalls. That was about 13 years ago. Now that I'm 26, I'm pretty much responsible for maintaining the daily operations of the entire ranch. I know that one day I will inherit it all. I hope that when I do, I'll be able to run it as well as my dad and his dad have done for the past two generations.

The ranch is spread out over 42 acres, so, needless to say, we have a lot of hired hands to keep the place running. Some of the help has been around for as long as I can remember. One of our most faithful employees is Old Man Tucker. Tucker believes there is nothing more honest than a hard day's work. Even though he is up in age, probably close to 65 years young, you can tell that his strong black body is rock-solid.

As summer approached, Old Man Tucker told my father and me that his grandson planned to spend a couple of months with him. He hadn't seen much of his grandson over the years, so he asked if it would be OK if he could bring him along and have him help out around the ranch. My dad and I thought it would be a great idea. Tucker told us that his grandson would be arriving in about a week. As Tucker was walking out I asked him, "So what's your grandson's name?"

He told us, "Wilson."

Wilson was an incredibly good-looking guy. And like Old Man Tucker, Wilson had his granddad's body. He stood about 6 feet tall and had muscles that just wouldn't quit. His skin was a smooth dark chocolate brown. The first day he arrived, Wilson was wearing faded blue jeans that fit just perfectly around his tight ass. The jeans also gathered around his crotch just enough for you to be able to tell he owned one meaty cock. He was wearing a loose-fitting tank top, which exposed extremely developed, muscular arms. When he approached me confidently and extended his hand for a handshake, I couldn't help noticing his thickly muscled shoulders and lats.

It was all I could do the first couple of weeks to keep my mind on my daily routine and my eyes off Wilson. I guess that explains why I was careless one day when it was just the two of us out in the field training one of our horses. Wilson was riding Maggie, a strong quarter horse that took to him right away. I was riding Jonah. Jonah was a high-spirited horse that you had to watch at all times. Well, when I should have been keeping my eyes on Jonah instead of Wilson, the horse decided to throw me. The throw was pretty bad because when I was catapulted, I was a little too close to the wire fence that surrounded the training area. I caught a pretty bad gash right across my left forearm. I was surprised at the amount of blood that poured out and covered me in a matter of seconds.

Wilson rushed over, jumped off Maggie, and helped me up. He held me by the waist, looked at my arm, and could tell immediately that it wasn't just a minor paper cut. He held on to me firmly and said, "We better get you to the doctor!" I told him I was fine and that I could just go to the first-aid kit and wrap it and go to the hospital later. Wilson didn't think that it would be a good idea. I told him that he was overreacting. Of course, I was trying not to make such a big deal out of it because I was embarrassed by the whole ordeal. At that point Wilson grabbed Jonah and tied him to a fence and helped me up on the back of Maggie while he rode the two of us back to the stable. As I was riding behind Wilson with my chest pressed up against his back, I realized that I had never been so close to another man before in my life. I began to feel a little light-headed. I decided that the cut might be worse than I thought. When we got back to the stable, Wilson dismounted like a pro and helped me down. As soon as my feet hit the ground, everything became a blur, and the last thing I remember hearing was Wilson yelling, *"Trey!"*

When I came to, I could barely open my eyes. The light was so bright. I could just make out the image of my dad,

Old Man Tucker, and Wilson standing over me along with some other guy who must have been the doctor. The doctor told me I was pretty lucky that they had gotten me to the hospital when they did. Because if I had lost any more blood, I would have run into some serious problems. I later found out that right after I collapsed, Wilson threw me into my car and drove me to the hospital. He called my dad and Old Man Tucker from my car phone and told them to meet us at the hospital.

The doctor gave me 19 stitches and told me I had to take it easy for about a week. He asked if there would be someone who would be able to keep an eye on me to make sure that I wouldn't be alone in the event I experienced any more dizziness. Wilson spoke up right away. After the doctor made out a prescription and got me all cleaned up, he told me that I was free to leave. As I was getting up, I asked him if I really had to stay off my feet for a full week. The doctor looked me straight in the eye and said that I had to relax, adding, "Doctor's orders!"

Wilson volunteered to stay with me through the night in the loft apartment I had converted from an old storage space above one of our old equipment stables.

Being an only child, I was kind of used to having my own space. I'd never had a roommate. Even in college I was always fortunate enough to have my own dorm room or off-campus apartment. But for some reason I was kind of excited about sharing my place with Wilson. As Wilson drove my car back to the ranch, I couldn't keep my eyes off of his hands as they gripped the steering wheel. I also couldn't forget the feeling of his hands when he placed both of them on my waist after I was thrown from the horse. It was only the sound of his voice that brought me back to the present when he asked whether or not this was the first time I had ever had stitches. I told him it was. When I asked whether or not he had ever had any similar experiences, he told me that he grew up in a pretty rough neighborhood. Wilson also went on to explain how you had to act really tough even if you weren't. He said that he was really glad to be out of that scene. That's why going away to college was really important for Wilson. He took studying very seriously because he knew that he didn't want to go back to where he came from.

As he was finishing up his story, we arrived at the ranch. Wilson drove directly to the loft, threw the car into Park, and jumped out. I realized that he was trying to run around to the passenger's side to open the door for me only after I was already halfway out of the car. As I began to head up the stairs, pulling the keys out of my pocket, Wilson took them from me without saying a word. He raced up to unlock the door. I couldn't believe how he was taking care of me. Wilson made sure I was settled and had everything I needed. He told me that he had to go back and untie Jonah and return him to the stable. With that he bounded out the door and down the stairs. As I was sitting on the couch, I suddenly realized that I was completely wiped out. Before I knew it, I nodded off and slipped into a dream.

I was standing near the edge of a cliff. It was a dark and cloudy day. The wind was blowing from all directions. At first the south wind would blow so hard that I would stumble toward the edge. I was fighting against the wind. But it was no use. Then just as I was about to fall over the edge of the cliff, the north wind would suddenly carry me back away from the cliff's edge. This seemed to go on forever. With each gust of the south wind, I would get closer to the edge. I could see the rocks and other debris being swept over the edge. It was terrifying. I was afraid to look over the edge of the cliff. Every time I got too close, I would shut my eyes. Then, just as I felt the ground crumbling beneath my feet, I knew I was about to go over the edge. I opened my eyes in complete terror.

Suddenly I saw Wilson floating below me with wings outspread like a dark dove. He was completely naked. His muscular arms caught me. He pulled me close to his chest. Then, without saying a word, he kissed blond curls on the top of my head, and together we flew to what seemed to be an isolated island. The weather was warm, and the sun was bright. We landed on a beach of white sand. Wilson gently laid me on the beach and stood over me. I thanked him for saving my life. I told him I'd thought I was going to die up there all alone. Wilson looked me in the eye and told me I wasn't going to die because I wasn't alone. With that he leaned down and kissed me. I could feel his cock become thick and hard. His hands caressed my face. I ran my hands over his entire body. His wings expanded as he began to grind his rod against me. His tongue entwined with mine as I opened my eyes, only to see his closed and completely engulfed in passion. My dick became harder than iron. I thought I was going to blow my wad.

Just then the ground began to quake. But we didn't stop. Wilson began to tear away at my shirt. He ran his hands over my chest. Grabbing and kissing my body at a ferocious pace, Wilson suddenly shifted gears and began gently nibbling at my skin. I began to moan out loud. Then Wilson began calling my name. The ground began quaking violently. My come was closer and closer to exploding.

Suddenly Wilson's image began to recede into the distance. I reached out for him, longing desperately to hold him one last time. Yet the climax was still rushing for release within me. All of this continued as the ground around me began to crumble. I began to sink into the earth. Just then, as Wilson's winged image disappeared in the clouds above me, my rod exploded with columns of come. I uttered an agonizing moan that filled me with pleasure—and sorrow, because Wilson was no longer in my arms.

As the violent shaking continued, I suddenly heard my name erupt like a trumpet blast in my ear. I awoke with a jolt. Wilson was standing over me with both hands on my shoulders, looking down at my crotch. I was completely confused by this situation. It was a split second later that I realized I had been dreaming. As I shifted my body, I felt a wetness in the crotch of my pants. It was at that point that I realized exactly what Wilson was looking at. I glanced down only to see a huge wet spot, which made it obvious that I had just unloaded. Feeling horribly embarrassed, I turned beet-red. Wilson slowly raised his head and looked at me with a devilish smirk. Without a word he released my shoulders and walked to the kitchen, just off to the right of the living room area of the apartment.

I quickly moved to the bathroom and, without closing the door, kicked off my shoes, unbuckled my belt, and stripped out of my jeans and briefs. My pubic hair was completely covered in come. Standing in front of the sink in only a tight gray T-shirt (which showed off my well-defined pecs, if I do say so myself), I heard a firm yet soft voice behind me say, "Need some help cleanin' up there, buddy?" I looked up into the mirror above the sink to see that Wilson was standing behind me, bare-chested, his arms folded across his massive pecs. I couldn't say a word. After about five seconds of silence, Wilson said, "Yeah, I thought so."

With that, Wilson walked up directly behind me and wrapped his strong arms around my waist. I immediately felt his thick dick pressing between my butt cheeks. With deft fingers, Wilson, in one smooth motion, lifted my T-shirt above my head. Then he turned me around and kissed my chest and abs, moving irrevocably toward my come-drenched pubes. Once he arrived at this point of destination, he began to lap at my jizz like a man discovering an oasis after being stranded in the desert for two months.

After licking me dry, Wilson engulfed my swollen dick with his mouth and worked my cock head up and down, firing away like a brand-new piston in a '98 Corvette. I moved my hands over his massive back, savoring the feel of his bulging muscles as he flexed them for my pleasure. Within seconds I was ready to fire off another load. This time I was going to shoot into the back of his throat instead of wasting my come on faded denim. As I began to moan, Wilson realized it wasn't going to be long. With that, he grabbed my ass with both hands and pulled me closer to him. I began to buck wildly. I flung my head back, and then my world went completely dark. Maybe I passed out, or maybe I'd been transported to another plane. All I remember is seeing a vision of Wilson with his outspread wings returning to me, his naked body glistening like the sun.

When the climax subsided, my swollen dick still twitched with the afterglow of ecstasy. My entire body was so racked with pleasure that I could no longer stand. My knees suddenly gave way, and I collapsed on top of Wilson. This surprised him, and he lifted me up on his back and carried me over to the couch. As he laid me down, he looked into my eyes and said, "Well, I guess I'm going to have to spend more than just a few days looking after you."

"Yeah?" I replied.

"Yeah," Wilson continued. "I'm really going to have to make sure I monitor your physical activity and also make sure you get your rest. Remember, doctor's orders!"

S.R., Ferndale, Mich.

◆ First Taste of a Marine ◆

I was on my first overseas assignment and had been sent to Okinawa, Japan, with the Marine Corps. I'm a corpsman in the Navy and had been assigned to a Marine Corps unit. I'd been in Okinawa for six months and was getting really horny, especially on days of doing patrol torpedo coverage. Just the sight of all those tight asses and huge bulges being displayed in those green PT shorts would have been enough to bring any man to his knees.

Because of my horniness, I looked everywhere, basically, for action. I checked out all the bathrooms on base for writing on the walls that would at least give an indication of where to meet someone for action. No luck—there was not a single note. Next I checked out the steam room at the base gym, thinking there might be some action there. I was lucky to find anybody even in the steam room let alone someone to mess around with. So, basically, my sex life was looking pretty bleak.

One day I was in the base library working on my term paper for my nutrition course, and this really cute guy with the prettiest blue eyes was totally checking me out. At first I thought it must be my imagination. Then after about ten minutes he came up to me and sat down next to me and said, "Hello, my name is Major Finley, and I've been watching you. You have the cutest smile and the bluest eyes I've ever seen." I said, "Your eyes are just as nice, and my name is Donald. Nice to meet you."

After we talked for a while, he started to touch me under the table. Since things were getting a little out of hand, I told him to meet me outside to discuss where we should go. We decided to go to a beach called Trash Beach, a nearby make-out spot that is usually frequented by underage Japanese couples who want to have sex in their cars. The major and I drove in his car. On the way to the beach, he told me he was from Camp Hansen and that he had a wife and two kids. He told me that his wife wasn't satisfying him sexually and that he was more attracted to men.

We finally arrived at the beach. It was just starting to get dark, so we found this parking spot that was surrounded by trees. At first he seemed kind of nervous about our parking in that spot—I guess he was afraid someone might see us since there was still a lot of daylight. As he began to kiss me, he whispered, "Keep one eye open to watch for cars, OK?" I responded, "Yeah, whatever." Our kissing began to get out of control, especially since both of our hands started to explore each other.

The major suggested that we get into the backseat so that we would have more room to mess around in, so we did. We didn't get out of the car, though. We eased the seats back all the way and slid back. Then we popped the seats back in the upright position. This time he started to forcefully suck my face. I've never had a kiss where someone was sucking on my tongue like it was my dick.

Somehow we both managed to take off all of our clothes as we continued our passionate kiss fest. Next he worked his way to my ear and neck, giving me goose bumps all over. He seemed to really enjoy tonguing my ear because he seemed to do it forever. Eventually he made his way down to my nipples, where he started to lick, suck, and chew. As he started on my nipples, I grabbed his manhood with my hand. His dick was so hard and long that it reminded me of a policeman's nightstick. It was a lengthy ten inches, and he was oozing precome like a Popsicle that was melting in the hot summer sun. The faster I stroked his cock, the harder he chewed my nipples. It was almost as if we were in an endurance challenge, seeing who could turn on whom more. After a few minutes of fast stroking, he shot his first hot load. His come shot was extraordinary; he shot at least three feet. Unfortunately, the shot was stopped from going any farther by the windshield of his car.

Now it was his turn to service me. He grabbed my nine-inch tool and swallowed it whole, as if he were on a mission. The very first suck, he went all the way down to my balls. At that point I knew he was an expert cocksucker. He sucked my shaft, licked and sucked my balls, and tongued my ass, alternating as if he were reading my personal handbook on how to get me off. I exploded in almost no time, mainly due to the fact I hadn't had sex in six months. He swallowed my entire load down his hot, talented throat.

It was my turn to return the favor, so I reached down and attempted to deep-throat his huge organ, only to gag. At first I could go only about halfway down, mainly because his dick was so enormous. So then I basically tried to relax my throat muscles and tried to go down on it slowly. Well, this time I got all ten inches down my throat, but on the way up I started to gag. By this time I was determined to do it properly, so I kept trying. After about four or five slow attempts, I was finally ready to go faster. The more comfortable I got sucking him off, the more I added to his excitement. I sucked him and played with his balls, and then I would finger his ass while I was sucking his manhood. I realized he was getting close again, so I started to stroke him. He shot another huge load, this time shooting all over the ceiling of the car.

The major asked, "Have you ever been fucked?" I responded, "No, but you're fixing to tell me what it feels like." So he lifted his legs in the air, spread-eagle, and said, "Go ahead, sailor, fuck my ass!" He spit on his hand and rubbed the spit in his asshole repeatedly until he thought he would be ready for me. Meanwhile, I'm spitting on my dick to get it ready for his ass.

I raised his ass up higher so that I could get a better angle to slide my dick in. I slowly shoved it in his tight hole. He whimpered with delight as I began thrusting between his tight ass checks. The more I pumped, the more he moaned in delight. Eventually I slid all nine inches deep inside his firm, tight ass. I thrusted and pounded his ass in that same position for half an hour, then decided to finish him off doggy-style.

I had the major put his face against the window, ass in the air and knees on the backseat. Then I slid my throbbing cock in again, pulling him back toward me by pulling on his shoulders, making him feel my entire nine inches. I could tell by his resistance that he was hurting, so I backed off and gave him his choice of positions.

He wanted to sit on my dick and go at his own pace. I leaned back in the seat, and he straddled my ever-erect cock. He began slowly, easing my dick gently between his ass cheeks. The longer he was on top of me, the faster he went. He got me really close a couple of times, then realized I was about to come and would either slow down or completely stop till I recovered.

After about an hour of bumping and grinding, he finally got off me, and we both started masturbating each other. He waited for me to come so that we would come together. We both shot all over the back of the front seats, causing a huge mess all over the car.

As we both sat there, totally exhausted, he told me that he was driving his wife's car and that he had one hell of a mess to either clean up or explain. We both laughed about the fact that it was now too dark to see if we'd gotten all the come off the car. We still meet on a regular basis, but we don't do it in cars anymore.

D.C., San Diego, Calif.

◆ Glamour Boy ◆

For as long as I could remember, I'd had crushes on other men. And although I had fooled around with some of my friends when we were teenagers, by the time I entered college I still had never really been with a man. But having spent all my life reading about Dick and Jane and Mom and Dad and their dog and cat—the perfect nuclear family—I felt even then that I needed to do what was expected of me. So I joined a fraternity, started going out with a beautiful girl, and hoped that these hetero "emasculators" would straighten me out.

It didn't work out that way. After a while at UC, Santa Barbara, scornfully known as the "Ken and Barbie" campus of the University of California system, I finally had to come to terms with the fact that I would always be attracted to the Kens. Still, I figured that Lisa and I would get married and do the whole family thing and that I could keep my desires hidden. I mean, after all, as long as I knew about them, I could keep them under control, right?

Being in a fraternity had its ups and downs. One of the ups was having all of this young male flesh parading around all the time. One of the downs was that now that I knew what I liked, I thought I was the only homo in the house and that I had made a mistake that would last a lifetime. Of course, I had my suspicions about some of my brothers, but nothing had ever happened—until Robb.

Robb had pledged when I was a sophomore and he was a freshman. His nickname in the house was "Glamour Boy" because he was very tan, very built, and very glamorous. In short, he was a god. He was the kind of guy who always wore the right thing, drove the right car, and dated the right girl. I wanted to be that girl!

Robb and I got to be good friends, and since we both declared the same major at around the same time, we took quite a few classes together. Our girlfriends were both psychology majors, so they got to be friends as well. In fact, it was not long before the four of us became inseparable.

One night, after the final house meeting of the year, Robb and I were hanging out at his car in the house parking lot, just shooting the breeze, when he said he wanted to ask me something.

"Go ahead," I replied, clueless as to what he would ask.

"Well, it's kind of hard, but here goes: If you were at work and your male boss offered you a promotion, what would you do?"

"I'd take it, of course. Why?"

"OK, what if he offered it to you on certain conditions?"

"On what sort of conditions?" I asked, not sure what he meant.

"You know...cond-i-i-itions." He dragged the word out.

"Exactly how conditional do you mean?"

"Well, you know my boss is gay and that he has a thing for me, right?"

"Yeah, so? Did he tell you he would give you the promotion if you did something sexual in return? Is that what you're trying to say?"

"Uh-huh."

At this point Robb started to look scared, like maybe he he had said too much. I, on the other hand, was wishing that he would say a lot more.

"Let me just ask you this," I began. "Did you get the promotion?"

"Yes." His voice was almost a whisper.

"And you're telling me this to get my approval? My reaction? What?"

"Yes," he murmured again, not even looking at me.

Let me stop here and explain where I was at this particular moment in time. My dick was hard, I could hardly breathe, and my heart was pounding a million miles a minute. I had been waiting for this moment all my life. Not only was I hearing the words I had longed to hear, but they were coming from the man who had been the object of countless of my masturbatory fantasies. His was the face and body I conjured up while in bed with a woman, and here he was, telling me that, willing or not, he had done a guy. I wanted to know more.

"Wow. Did you like it?"

"Yeah, I did. He was really nice to me and said that he didn't want me to do anything more than I wanted to. Actually, I liked it a lot!" As Robb saw that I was not going to hit him or run and tell all the other guys, his voice returned to normal, and he began to sound a bit more enthusiastic. I felt like it was my move.

"Robb, now let me ask you something," I said. "If I were your boss and offered you that promotion on the same condition, would you have a better job right now?"

"Of course!" he said, sounding surprised. "Kevin's just my boss, and you're my bro! You wanna see what it's like?"

"You mean…you and me?" I was more than dumbfounded.

"Yeah! But we have to go to my place. I really don't think that here is the safest place to play."

Robb lived in a house about three miles off campus. He had two roommates, but they had already gone home for the summer. We entered the house rather tentatively and walked to the living room. Only the outside patio light was on, and we just stood there, neither of us wanting to make the first move. Finally I said, "Well, you're the one with the experience. What do we do?"

Robb took a step toward me and moved his arms ever so slowly into an embrace. When we finally kissed, it was like he was the missing piece to a puzzle I had been unable to solve my entire life. It felt right, and it worked like magic. There was none of that awkward bumping of noses until the "right" position was reached; we fit together well, our mouths opening at the same time to taste each other's tongues, which we frantically swirled together. At some point our shirts came off, and I saw the chest that I had come to know so well from volleyball games and barbecues on the beach. I was seeing it differently, though, because this time I could look rather that glance. And I could touch.

Robb worked out regularly but not obsessively, and his chest was well-defined, with whorls of hair surrounding his nipples. The hair tapered off to a treasure trail leading down his abdomen to the top of his shorts. Not yet knowing the power behind a man's nipples, I glossed over them in search of his penis, which I found when it bumped my chin much sooner that I thought it would on my tongue trip down his body. I pulled down his shorts and stood back. His dick was throbbing and standing out almost straight out from his body. It was long but with average thickness. He had a thick brown bush that traveled south to his balls, which were not too large but certainly not too small, just the right size to get both in your mouth at the same time, which was definitely on my list of priorities.

Robb grabbed my hands, pulled me up, and undressed me. By the time he got my boxers off, they were soaked with precome. I tend to leak more when I'm in that semi-erect state, which I had been while talking to him through-out the evening. Now my prick stood straight out from my body, with that big Y-shaped vein on top pulsing. I could feel every hair on my body standing on end. We kissed again, this time with our wet dicks rubbing against each other. We lay down on the living room carpet and kissed some more, rolling around in the shaggy pile. Our hips were thrusting, humping, and I could feel our pubes getting slicker and slicker with precome. We were panting now, getting closer and closer to climax. I wanted to come, but there was something I wanted even more: I wanted to taste Robb's dick. I pulled away from him and pushed him onto his back on the floor. I grabbed his hard dick and put my mouth over the head. I didn't know what to expect, but it was wonderful! I loved the taste, the way it felt in my mouth, and everything else about it. It had a salty taste, which I attributed to our precome. I went farther down and was amazed by how alive it felt. Or maybe it was that the farther down I went, the more Robb would squirm. From that and his moaning—or maybe from what he was saying—I knew I was doing a good job.

"Oh, yeah, suck my dick! You do it so well! So much better than Denise! Suck it!"

That was all I needed to hear—that I sucked dick better than his girlfriend. Let me tell you, I went to town. Although I couldn't get his big meat all the way down my throat without gagging, I figured out how to use my hand on the part that was outside my mouth. Then Robb taught me about the pleasure of sucking a man's balls. I began by licking, then moved swiftly to giving them an out-and-out tongue bath, rolling the balls around in my mouth, pulling the hairs with my teeth.

After a while Robb decided that it was my turn. He had me lie back as he leaned over and began to kiss me. As he kissed he played with my nipples. This was a first—finally I knew what they were for! The nerves in them seemed directly connected to my crotch. As his tongue flicked over them, making them harder than they'd ever been, I began to get sensations all over my body like I had never experienced before. I felt like I was alive, electric, like I was just on the verge of feeling really tickled but not quite there. It was incredible. His mouth went down my body, stopping at my other nipple and belly button on the way. When he got to my dick, there was no hesitation. He took it all the way down in one gulp, which tells you that either I am of average proportions or he had a large gullet. I prefer to believe it was the latter. I gasped and tensed; I'd never felt anything like that before. He was right—this was better than any girlfriend!

As his head moved up and down, faster and faster, the realization that I had sucked Robb's dick and now he was sucking mine pushed me over the edge. I arched my back, moaned that I was coming, and tried to pry Robb's head from my dick. At least I tried. It was too late, and I shot my entire load down his throat. I don't think he expected that much because he came off my dick coughing and sputtering yet still licking come from his lips.

He kissed me, passing some of my load back to me. That turned me on so much, I pushed him down and returned the favor—or at least tried to. He was so close that as soon as I got his dick in my mouth, he came. A lot. It spilled everywhere. When he was done, we began to smile, then laugh.

Robb and I spent the night sleeping together and sucking each other, coming one more time as the sun came up.

After that, Robb and I got together as often as we could, frequently ending up at my new studio apartment after drunken parties at the house. Robb was never really able to come out of the closet. He and his girlfriend still dated, although she acknowledged his secret sexuality as much as I did. She actually did know about us but never spoke of it. It got to the point where the three of us would go out to the gay bar in town. He and I would check out the dudes, and she would check out the women.

My girlfriend, Lisa, and I eventually broke up under some false pretense. When I finally came out to her over a year later, she told me that she had known a year and a half before we broke up. In fact, almost everyone I came out to said pretty much the same thing, including my frat brothers. They really did provide me with support in my coming-out. Today, ten years later, I still have close ties to my fraternity and my brothers, although some are just a little closer than others.

I.F., Los Angeles, Calif.

◆ Hard-on Hotel ◆

When I was doing a lot of traveling, I found out early on that many married men who stay in the better hotels are interested in meeting other males because they do not want to take chances with prostitutes (or spend money on them).

Some years ago, while flying back home from the Carolinas, I had to spend the night in Atlanta because the weather had turned bad. The airline put me up at the airport Hilton. That night in the bar, I took the stool next to one of the most beautiful women I had ever seen—truly lovely. She was dressed in simple black, with a strand of pearls and white gloves, and wore her hair in a chignon. She was a patrician type of female, something like Grace Kelly.

After some minutes she slid off the stool and left. I figured she was going to powder her nose. The man she was with saw me, in the mirror, staring at her and grinned. I was embarrassed and commented that he had an exceptionally beautiful wife. He laughed, slid onto the stool she had left, and told me in a low voice that she was not his wife, only a "$100-a-night whore."

I was really surprised and replied that she was probably worth every penny. He snorted and said that rather than spend $5 getting laid by a prostitute, he would rather go to bed with another guy. And then his knee connected with mine. With as straight a face as I could manage, I said that, in fact, I would too.

Not more than ten minutes passed before we were in his room, undressing each other. We stood face-to-face, kissing and stroking each other's cock. He did not resist at all when I maneuvered him down on the bed, flat on his back. I then mounted him and lined my cock up on his, kissing him all the while.

By dawn I had come at least five times just by rubbing against him. As masculine as this married guy was, he never once gave any indication he would like to do it riding on top. As strange as it seems, I have met a lot of masculine married males who, for one reason or another, prefer to be on the bottom while rubbing bodies with another male. That has always been fine with me!

There are, of course, exceptions. I met one the next day at the same hotel. I had to stay overnight an extra day because of inclement weather. My friend of the night before decided to take a taxi into downtown Atlanta and visit some friends, so I was alone again. En route to the restaurant for breakfast, I stopped at the reception desk and overheard a girl behind the counter talking with an airline captain. What I heard jolted me: "Should I arrange for a girl or a young man this time, Captain?"

She said it with a smile. He shook his head, still writing on the check-in form, saying he was tired and all he wanted right then was some sleep. She turned away for a moment, and he looked up and saw me staring at him. I guess I had a stupid look on my face. And more than likely, he could see plainly enough from my expression that, given half a chance, I would hop into bed with him myself.

To my surprise, he came into the restaurant about 15 minutes later. I glanced up from my paper and saw him at the entrance looking my way. He half grinned, and I responded by gesturing to the vacant chair across from me.

As much as that skipper needed rest, he proved to be a tiger who still had a lot of reserve energy once we hit the mattress. I was flat on my back before I knew what was happening. He liked doing it by planting his cock (which was as hard as a tire iron) between my legs and working it up and down like a piston. We were stuck together, flesh to flesh, from mouth to toe. He fuck-rubbed his entire hairy body down hard on my own. I could feel damn near every muscle in his body.

When he finally exploded and collapsed, I hung on to him. As tall as he was, he was very lean and lithe, and his weight felt good on me. Long after he had stopped moving, I savored the pleasure of his cock driving between my thighs and his belly rubbing against mine. He fell asleep on top of me, and after a while I dozed off.

Some time before noon, I woke up to find him fuck-rubbing me again. He had his cock lined up on mine and his hands underneath my buttocks. This time it lasted longer and was even better.

J.C., Erie, Pa.

• He Lays More Than Carpet •

My sister had called me earlier that morning wanting to know if I could come over and help her install a new carpet. I told her I didn't know a lot about laying carpet, but I'd help all I could.

When I pulled up an hour later and went inside, there was a house full of people. They were all sitting around getting high and drinking beer. I made sure to sit down so I could keep my eyes on Jackie. I hadn't seen him in a few years, but one thing was for sure: I still envied his wife for having the opportunity to get Jackie to work her over with his big dick anytime she wanted it. I'd heard her bragging a few years back about how big his dick was.

When we started laying carpet, everyone left except me, Jackie, his wife, and my sister. While we were working, I bumped into Jackie every chance I could. He just joked around and kept looking up, laughing every time he caught me staring between his legs. No one knows I like men, at least not my family and friends, but I was sure he could tell what I wanted.

When we got finished, I had to get home. I told everyone good-bye and walked out to my truck. Jackie walked out with me and shook my hand, thanking me for the help with the carpet. I told him it was good seeing him again and to catch up with me sometime soon and we'd get drunk or high. He asked me for my phone number and directions to my house. I wrote it out in big numbers and told him to be sure to get by soon.

Saturday night around 10 my phone rang. It was Jackie! He said, "I've got a few joints and a bottle of whiskey and was wondering if you were up to me dropping by shortly."

I said, "Sure!" I was nervous as hell, just wondering if he was going to feed me that big dick of his. As bad as I wanted him, I knew I'd have to let Jackie make the first move. I went to the bathroom and greased up my asshole really good. I just wanted to be prepared for a good hard fucking.

He knocked on my door, and when I let him in, I could tell he was pretty drunk. He handed me a bottle and told me to fix him a drink while he rolled up a joint. I fixed both of us a drink and went and sat down by him on the couch. We smoked the joint he had rolled, and every time he passed it to me, I made more contact than normal. Every time I touched his hand, my asshole would start twitching. Jackie looked at me slowly and asked, "Why did you want me to come over?"

"I just did," I said.

He stood up, grabbed his crotch, and said, "This is what you want, isn't it?"

I couldn't utter a single word. I just watched as he pulled down his pants and started pulling on his dick. After a few strokes he moved his hand away, and his dick was at half-mast. It was really something, all ten thick inches of it. The head was still half covered. I grabbed him by the base of that big dick and pulled him toward me. I started licking the purple head, and then I skinned it back and swallowed as much of it as I could. It took some doing, but before long I had all of his massive dick down my throat and his big balls slapping my chin.

I was really working on Jackie's dick, and he was loving it. He was bucking and moaning. I knew he wasn't far from coming, so I came off his dick and just stared at it for a few minutes. I quickly took off my pants and pulled Jackie my way. His dick was hard as a rock as I guided it to my tight little hole. Once he had slipped the head in and let my asshole get used to the girth of his fat dick, he said, "Hold on, because I'm fixing to tear that asshole up for you." Then he drove it home.

It hurt for a few strokes, then I started throwing my ass at him hard, wanting to make him like it so he'd come back for more. He was running that dick in and out of my asshole like a piston, and I was saying, "Give it to me, give me all that big dick," and he was too. He fell forward, and I could feel his breath on my neck. I grabbed the cheeks of his ass and pulled him toward me. When I felt his hot juice filling up my insides, my dick just erupted, covering my belly with come.

Jackie collapsed on me and said, "Damn, that's some good fucking pussy, baby."

Well, I made him like it, just like I'd hoped to. I look forward to having him drop by anytime. And he does come by every chance he gets.

R.S., Mobile, Ala.

◆ High on the Coast ◆

At first, Mario's hand on my leg felt like nothing more than the easy familiarity of an old friend. It was the girls' turn to drive, and he and I had stretched out as best we could on the backseat of my old Coupe de Ville. We'd already driven 200 miles up the Pacific Coast Highway and had about 50 more to go before we reached the turnoff to the mountain cabin among the redwoods.

I had most of the seat. Mario was lying partly on the two double sleeping bags in the space between the backseat and front seats. My Vera was driving, and his Trixie was in the passenger seat delivering a steady stream of conversation that became a kind of background music lulling us to sleep.

I like the feel of Mario crowding me. We hadn't seen one another since graduation years before. He'd stayed in the Midwest, and I'd come out to California. I'd really missed his rugged Italian good looks, and when he phoned to tell me they'd be flying out, I was excited. Being bigger, stronger, and more extroverted than me, he had been a kind of big brother to me in our dorm. When he and Trixie suggested we spend a couple of days with them in the Santa Cruz Mountains, I jumped at the chance.

We had a blanket over us, and it was getting dark out. Mario seemed to be asleep, but every time the car swung around a curve his body pressed a little more against mine and his hand inched farther up the inner side of my left leg. It was just where the long, tough thigh muscle swells out from the softer flesh below. I began to be conscious of, and then acutely concerned about, his hand's progress.

At first I didn't think he was doing this on purpose. He'd always been a hands-on kind of guy—lots of butt-slapping and goosing and comradely hugging—but it had all been completely macho. I'd been the one to sneak glances at his furry muscularity when he went around the room unselfconsciously naked and to go warm all over when he casually touched me.

I was beginning to feel my cock press uncomfortably against the soft fabric of my worn-out blue jeans. When his hand reached the tear in the cloth about three inches from my crotch and I felt his fingers on my bare flesh, I had to slip my hand under my waistband and pull my cock up so that it would have room to expand along the crease between my belly and thigh.

My heart began to pound. I was scared silly but at the same time intensely aroused to think that we might be making out while the girls were only two feet away. All this time I was still not absolutely sure Mario was even awake. But when he unbuttoned the top of my jeans and unzipped me, there could no longer be any doubt: He was making a move on me!

And having been so overt, he now knew that I knew and that I was acquiescing. He took my right hand and drew it to his crotch, where the big, thick cock I had always been so turned on by was now as hard as an ax handle under the soft cotton of his jeans.

I thought in a panic, *I can quit now and act innocent, not once I start pulling that zipper.* With a sigh I yielded and pulled it. His cock sprang out and was instantly in my hand, a hard, very warm velvety shaft that jerked against my palm and fingers.

At the same moment, he took hold of my cock, his grip strong and firm, so unlike the soft, feminine touch of my wife's fingers. It was the grip of a man taking charge, and I felt an intense gratification in submitting to him.

His hand left my cock and stroked my balls. I spread my legs to let him in, and he cupped my balls while with his middle finger he traced a line back to my asshole, which he rubbed seductively. I felt my sphincter yield, and the finger slid in. He began to stroke the wall of my rectum, and I lost all control.

As I felt the pressure of my orgasm beginning to mount in my crotch, I wondered desperately how I could get a handkerchief out in time to catch my come. But Mario seemed to sense my climax on its way and suddenly plunged his face down into my crotch and took my cock in his mouth. I felt myself shooting hard enough to make me grit my teeth. Mario swallowed it all and then milked my cock of its remaining ooze and licked it up.

When he moved back up on me, he had wrapped his cock in a bandanna, and he lay on top of me, his hard shaft squeezed between our bare bellies, and humped against my body until he came. I felt the warm come seeping through the bandanna, drying on my stomach. He licked his come from the bandanna and planted his lips on mine, and I tasted the soft, warm fluid sliding into my mouth.

"I've always wanted to do that, blondie," he whispered, his lips warm against my ear.

The intensity of my excitement had blotted out everything else around me. As I came down from this high, I could hear Trixie still rattling on. We had the night ahead of us, and I knew with an exhilarating certainty that my old buddy would be inside me sometime during it.

P.N., San Luis Obispo, Calif.

◆ In the Crease ◆

"*Loose, loose, loose!*" the ref yelled. Me and Konawalchek had locked sticks together. I was so focused on getting free and slapping the puck into the net, I didn't even see him drop his gloves. But—*wham!*—the next thing I knew, I was flat on my back on the ice.

That's college hockey for you. It's fast and furious, and if you're anything less than tough as shit, you're never gonna make it. Konawalchek's sucker punch came when no one was looking, no one except for my buddy and offensive lineman, Jimmy, who was the toughest of all. He was our team's enforcer—you know, the big, bad guy on every roster who's taller and meaner than anyone else. The guy nobody messes with. The first one to throw down the gloves and fire off the punches. It just so happened that Jimmy, our team's mean motherfucker, also happened to be my best friend and roommate in college. As I scrambled back to my skates, shaking the stars out of my head, I heard the ref's whistle.

Jimmy was punching away, as was Konawalchek. They matched each other, blow for blow, while all the guys in the black-and-white stripes kept trying to separate them. But soon Konawalchek's hockey jersey and shoulder pads were twisted around his neck. Jimmy had the other guy down on his back. The double penalty put four men from both teams on the ice and Konawalchek and Jimmy in the penalty box once the fight ended. I knew Jimmy hadn't just done it for the team. He'd taken one for me.

Yeah, ice hockey's a tough game, the *toughest.* It's all speed and sweat, blood and balls. You gotta have ice in your veins colder than what you play on if you want to survive the sport, but sometimes something happens, and you and your teammates get closer than guys are suppose to.

It happened to me that night—with Jimmy.

Maybe I've had it bad for him from the start, but I knew something was different after the game. Not in Jimmy; he stood over six feet tall, with jet-black hair and warm, dark eyes, the stubble of a goatee that never got too full or long, and the kind of body, like mine, from a lifetime of being an athlete. Summer baseball and spring lacrosse had pumped his quads and calves full and solid. He had strong biceps and a ropy, defined abdomen. Jimmy didn't have much hair up top—just nice armpits and a ring of it around his belly button. But from the waist down, he was pure Canadian grizzly. Plenty of short black hair on his legs, butt, and the tops of his long, flat toes. He had a full bush, and some of that hair ran along the long, slender sides of his cock as well as on the low-dangling balls that made Jimmy *Jimmy.*

What changed was *me*. Jimmy and I'd roomed together since freshman year at college, so I already knew what it was like to see him in action, either banging one of his girlfriends or going at it solo, stroking his slender seven-incher late at night when he thought I was asleep or early, before class, when he thought I wasn't yet awake. There were even times when he jacked it openly in front of me, and I'd join in, him on his side of the room, me on mine in my bed, neither of us ever talking about it 'cause that wasn't something guys did.

At least not until that night, after the game, after the locker room, after lights-out in the hotel room we shared, while beyond the window the snow was coming down hard. But the warm, comforting sound of my buddy's snores lit some fire deep inside me, melting the ice in my blood. I guess I'd always secretly wanted something more from my team's enforcer. Even when I slipped out of my sweat-soaked covers onto the carpeted floor between our beds, I didn't believe it or that I'd do it. The hard-on in my mid-lengths wouldn't go down, no matter how many times I'd stroked it, spurred on like tribal drumbeats by the deep grunts of Jimmy's snoring. I'd already dumped two loads of spunk onto the sheets. The clock read just shy of 2 in the morning, and I was wide awake, harder beside Jimmy than my dick's ever been.

Jimmy's equipment bag lay at the foot of his bed. I carefully snuck the zipper down in the darkness and fished out his cup, hoping the smell of his cock, the stink of his dirty underwear and socks, might be enough to satisfy me. I fished out his jock, ran the musky, moist cotton over my nose and mouth. I even licked the plastic where his sweaty cock and nuts had rested, but that only teased my hunger for the real thing.

You're a cocksucker, dude, a voice in my head told me. *No,* I spat back. *I'm Jimmy's cocksucker...*

He was snoring deeply, crashed out on his back in a pair of white briefs, his bared chest, legs, and big jock feet causing my heart to beat faster as I wrestled with the danger of what I wanted so badly from him. If Jimmy caught me, he'd most likely kick my ass. I might get thrown off the team, maybe forced out of school if the guys found out. Worse, I'd lose the best friend I'd ever had, the dude who'd guarded my ass, if he woke up to find my mouth wrapped around his stick.

But, *fuck*—I had to touch it, feel it, suck it...

Putting my hand down on the hot, meaty tent in Jimmy's underwear seemed to take forever. The clock read past 2. Before I could talk myself out of it, I had a finger inside the piss slit of his white briefs and was touching the hot, soft, hairy meat of one of Jimmy's nuts. Soon I had two fingers, then three, through the crease, and I was rubbing the soft head of his penis. I wiggled his cock out. The arrow-shaped knob trembled with my shaking fingertips. I leaned down, opened my mouth, and—still in disbelief—sucked the fleshy head between my lips. For the first time, I tasted Jimmy's manhood.

It was warm and salty, musky and clean at the same time.

I didn't even know what I was doing, but somehow I think every dude has some idea of hot to suck cock. We learn it from our girlfriends, but more, I guess, just from *having* a cock and realizing how we like to have it treated. I took Jimmy's meat down to his nuts, buried my nose in the crisp, course shag sticking out of his briefs, and sucked like my life depended on it. The hard-on in my own briefs pushed painfully against the elastic waistband. I was just about to whip my own stick out of my underwear—and the big, hairy puck-nuts from Jimmy's—when he suddenly grunted and shifted on the bed. I spit out Jimmy's cock and hit the deck, sure I'd been found out, ready to hang up my skates and kiss what used to be my straight man's ass good-bye.

Instead, Jimmy's snores grew deeper. When I looked up, he'd spread both his legs and his arms. His right hand lay flopped over the edge of the bed perilously close to me. The left he'd slid unconsciously into his briefs and had wiggled his meaty stick back in through the piss hole.

I would have crashed back onto my bed, but that quick taste of Jimmy's cock proved too addictive. I needed it, needed it *bad.* After a few minutes that felt like hours, I resumed my position on my knees at the side of the bed and reached for the bulge in his underwear. Even in the poor light, I could see Jimmy's hand, stuck down in his briefs, groping his hog and balls. The forest of black pubic hair was visible on either side of his wrist, and when I pulled on his waistband, the front of his underwear slid down easily over his knuckles. In fact, his feeling himself up had made my task quicker to accomplish. I tucked his tight-whites under his low-hangers. All that remained now was to get between his fingers and free that hot cock. I carefully lifted Jimmy's left thumb. Then I found something out.

"Aw, fuck..." I whispered.

Jimmy had popped a hard-on in his sleep!

As carefully as I could, I pulled the stiff stick toward me, aiming the head at my mouth. Once I had the cap of his stick and the first inch of its handle on top of my tongue, I clamped down hard and sucked his dick the rest of the way out from under his hand. Gulping on Jimmy soft had been one thing, but having him hard in my mouth was another. His cock had a strange, rubbery feel to it. It pushed against my tongue. I could feel the fucking thing rising to the occasion! I lowered closer. The action pressed Jimmy's free right hand into my pouch. I almost blew right then and there just by the brush of his knuckles.

Lifting my leg, I pulled my underwear off my thigh, baring my nuts. I guided Jimmy's sleeping hand into my shorts and, once there, carefully wrapped his fingers around my stick. With his unintentionally pumping my dick and my going crazy on Jimmy's cock, I was beyond caring, beyond worrying. It all felt so good, so right.

It didn't sink in at first when Jimmy stopped snoring. Then I heard him growl, right about the same time I tasted something thick and salty on my tongue.

His come! I told myself, and I started sucking faster, harder.

Jimmy's left foot suddenly skidded across the sheets as he spread his legs. He coughed, then groaned. The fingers in my underwear flexed on their own. I in turn moaned around Jimmy's cock just as I heard an "Aw, fuck!" from the head of the bed. Come hell or high water, I had to have his load. He was so close that even when he started awake and growled out an angry "What the fuck!" I didn't stop, didn't pull away. I'd already crossed the blue line. It was power-play time, and I was in the crease. Instead of giving up, I skated on, sucked harder, and scored as the first blast of come hit the roof of my mouth.

But instead of kicking my ass like I'd expected my hockey hero to do, the hand in my underwear started beating on its own. He other hand gripped the back of my head.

Jimmy let out a painful howl, then raised his concrete ass off the bed, burying his stick deeper in my mouth. His come came in spurts, heavy and full, a taste unlike anything else I'd ever tasted. I gulped him instinctively to stop from gagging on the flood of jizz. Jimmy's rough grip on the back of my head and the seed shooting in my mouth pushed me over the edge. I felt the strength leave my legs as a blast of warmth flooded my mid-lengths.

Jimmy sighed and settled back on the bed, breathing heavily. Saying nothing, he pulled his hand from my shorts and brought the sticky mess to my face. Just as wordlessly I lapped his fingers clean. I'd no sooner licked his thumb—waiting for the other skate to fall—when Jimmy's hand cupped the back of my head to give me a victory pat. Next he pulled me into bed with him. Our bodies pressed together in the hot, sour air.

"Thanks, dude," he growled, putting that strong arm of his around me, holding me tight. We slept the rest of the night together in his bed, and nothing between us changed—except that Jimmy stopped jacking off in secret.

From that night on and to this very day, he's had me to take care of him, and, man—neither of us could be more stoked about it.

G.N., Atkinson, N.H.

◆ Knee-jerk Reaction ◆

Most guys I know spent their teens and early 20s trying to earn as much money as they could and scoring as often as possible. A lot of us came into our own once we hit our late 20s and learned that there was a lot more to life than that.

That's what happened to me and my good buddy Steve in 1994 during a long, hot summer when we both were going nowhere, working a nowhere job. Neither of us had gone to college. We knew what we wanted, just not how to get it. See, I met Steve earlier that year, and to say we became fast friends is an understatement. I'd already been working in the warehouse for two years by the time he got hired. But I knew right away he was genuine and cool and that we were going to be the best of buddies. He didn't let me down.

Understand, I'm not bad to look at. Six feet tall. Short

dark hair buzzed close and clean. Green eyes—green like emeralds—big hands, big feet, moderately hairy, pretty solid, about 180. Just an average Joe who always wondered what it would be like to score with another guy but who'd been too chicken to try it up to that point. I was trying to go somewhere too but was trapped in a nowhere job.

The day Steve came walking into the warehouse, he was dressed in blue jeans, old construction boots, and a tight-fitting T-shirt that clearly showed off the time he was spending at the gym. His arms, bare and covered in golden hair, were pumped and solid. You couldn't tell he was balding, even for a guy of 25, by the way he kept his head shaved down to a length that would have given George Clooney a run for the money. Steve wasn't handsome by male-model standards, just good-looking because of his masculinity, his genuineness, and the fact that he had no clue about what a good guy he really was.

The warehouse boss asked me to show Steve the ropes, which meant half an hour of brainless yammering on how to pick and stack the merchandise. A real mental challenge, I explained to him. We started to laugh and just sort of hit if off. By the end of the day I told him what it was I really wanted to do with my life. I'm not sure why. In a nowhere job you don't think about the future, or you might remember how fast the clock is ticking, even if it drags like a snail on the warehouse wall. Steve admitted to me he had an identical dream—to go to school, get his degree, then work in a job he could actually go somewhere with. Right after that he told me he'd just broken up with his girlfriend, who was herself off to school. That's how it all started.

I can't say I considered myself *gay* before that summer; I'd always wondered what it would be like to have sex with another man, but I didn't start craving it until Steve and I grew close, both during and after work. We'd get together and watch baseball, order a pizza, hang out and talk about how we were going to get free of our shitty jobs with the shitty pay and move on with our lives.

One Friday night Steve and I were at his small apartment. It was a one-room studio with a bed, chair, kitchenette, and bathroom. We were going to stay together to watch the game, but we had a few hours to kill until the national anthem, so we kicked back, downed some cold Cokes, and started talking again about college.

"Fall's gonna come quick," I'd said. "One more reminder of what we gotta do if we want to move on."

I don't know how, exactly, the conversation got on the subject of sex. Steve had told me that, except for his girlfriend, he hadn't had much experience with women. As he wiggled out of his work boots and sat on the edge of his bed, I told him that would all change in college.

"There's no teacher like experience," I said.

"Wish it was the fall," Steve joked, flexing his toes in his white socks like a contented cat.

Sitting in the big easy chair beside his bed, I gave his nearest foot a good-natured punch. "Not just girls," I told him. "You'll have your choice of guys, to boot."

Steve shrugged and shook his head. "What—?"

"*Dudes,* man. A lot of guys experiment with other guys in college."

"I ain't sucking no man's dick," Steve laughed.

"You don't got to," I said. "But you'll find plenty of guys who'll be happy to suck *yours*."

"Know where I can get some?" he asked, adding a nervous laugh to the question.

"Yeah, *right here*," I joked.

It had to have been a knee-jerk reaction—his asking, my answering. But while we both laughed, Steve went quiet after that. The only sound came from his breathing, conspicuously loud even with the TV on in the background as he flipped channels waiting for the game to come on. Each *thunk* from the tube caused my heart to beat faster. I'm not sure why I didn't stop there, because it was obvious how uncomfortable he was. Now I'm glad I didn't.

"You know," I said, sure my ticker was going to blow up in my chest, "I've heard nobody gives better head than another guy."

"I heard that too," Steve said, smirking. "Too bad we don't know any gay guys."

Before I could talk myself out of it, I picked up Steve's left foot, hefting the heavy, muscled calf onto my knee, and began to massage the damp cotton covering his toes. Steve let out a groan, but he didn't resist my probing fingers. In fact, when I looked up, his eyes had shut tightly, and the rest of his body had gone rigid, paralyzed. He let out a grunt and shook his head as I played with his toes with one hand and rubbed his sole with the other.

"*Mmm...*" he growled. "That feels good."

Taking his cue, I slid my hands into the pant leg of his jeans and slipped the sock down, off his ankle. Holding him by his hairy calf, I kissed his foot, loving the feel and taste of another man. Once I had spit-shined the left, I moved on to the right, enjoying the scratchiness and warmth of my best friend's body.

When I'd finished worshiping his right foot, I looked up. Steve's eyes were still clamped shut, his body rigid. The only sign of life came from the lump in his jeans between his legs. It was all I needed to see to know that everything was OK. Sliding off the chair and between Steve's outstretched legs, I could feel his gym-pumped muscles flexing inside his jeans. He didn't stop me when I put my hand on the full pouch of his groin. I gave it a squeeze and felt the hard lump of his cock and the meaty fullness of his nuts logroll beneath my fingers.

"Oh, man," Steve groaned.

Releasing his lump, I reached up, hands shaking, and fumbled with his belt buckle. By the time I'd started worming his zipper down, a dark, sticky ring of precome had stained the crotch of his jeans. It told me he wanted it as bad as I did, even if he had started to protest.

"I don't know," he growled, an arm draped over his eyes. "Don't know if we should be doing this..."

"Sure you do," I growled back, giving his jeans and boxers a firm yank that bared his straining erection. *"And sure we should."* I tugged the clothes off his sexy feet, then went back up to his cock, which I mentally measured at about six inches. Real fat, with two shaved nuts hanging under the trim triangle of dark blond peach fuzz. Steve still smelled like work—sweaty and crisp and a little musky from what I guessed to be the load he must have shot that morning and left in his boxers.

"Fuck, Stevie," I huffed. Then I ran my nose over his nuts, sniffing and lapping at the man sweat infusing his heavy sac. After playing with his balls and lifting them up, I tongue-fucked his asshole. Steve's had a sprout of dark blond hair around it. I licked his inner thigh, tasted the heady musk of his trimmed bush, all the while giving his cock some firm, upward strokes.

"Feels nice, guy," Steve sputtered. His handsome face was still concealed behind his arm. As I went down on his cock, sucking the wet, straining head into my mouth, I reached up and took hold of his arm, pulling it off his face. I wanted him to see what was going on.

Through slitted eyes he watched me do for him what only his girlfriend had done in the past. I loved the taste of him, the salty-sweet syrup of his precome. I got off on the feel of his balls, playing with them while my other hand rubbed his hairy butt. I even teased his hole with my thumb, massaging the moist, velvety terrain with small circular movements.

Steve, in turn, loved my attention so much that he became wide-eyed with wonder. He was panting hard, each muscle of his sculpted body rippling beneath me. He spread his legs on instinct, so I slid a finger into his hot, hairy asshole. This pushed Steve over the edge.

"I'm coming...!" he grunted. His cock seemed to double in size in my mouth, firing off one, two, half a dozen steady shots of his man juice. I had to swallow to keep up with him. When he finally stopped spraying, Steve slumped down on the bed. I still had some of his jizz left in my mouth, and I boldly went up to kiss him.

"No way, man," he said, resisting.

But he wasn't half as resistant to kiss me as he was to return the favor. I had my cock out of my jeans and aimed right at his face.

"Get the fuck out of here!" Steve said, chuckling, and pushed me away.

"Do it!" I ordered. Soon we were wrestling on the bed, our clothes strewn on the floor, the first inning of the ball game just getting under way.

Yeah, I'll admit it—I made him taste his own load. I kissed him. Even got him to suck cock that night.

Steve went away that fall, and we lost contact after I too moved out of state and on campus. While I'm sure he's got a girlfriend, I can't help wondering sometimes if he's been practicing in college what he learned that night with me—two regular Joes who found themselves on a hot summer night and realized they were *somebody*.

G.N., Atkinson, N.H.

◆ Let's Make a Deal ◆

A year or so ago I became friends with a guy from the gym where I work out. At 22, he was 16 years younger than I, and his buff 6-foot-3 frame towered over my meager 5-foot-9 runner's build. Tony had thick, wavy jet-black hair; big brown eyes; thick, luscious lips; and—usually—a day's worth of beard. Since he was a noncompetitive bodybuilder, he had chosen to retain his chest and abdominal hair—a very sexy look compared to the other, smoother bodybuilders. We worked out together and got together once a week for beers, and it soon became evident that Tony was all man, very much into sports, very much into women—very straight.

At first Tony was very uncomfortable with my being gay, uncomfortable that a fag was spotting him, uncomfortable that this fag saw him in loose tank tops and spandex shorts that left very little to the imagination. Sure, I lusted after him, even shot a few loads with him in mind, but our friendship was too important to me to ever consider trying to get him in bed.

One of the things I found out about Tony was that he has a great eye for detail and had developed a number of landscape designs in my neighborhood. Since I was lacking greenery around my pool area, I enlisted Tony to help give me some ideas about what I could do. He quickly sketched out a plan, and I gave him the go-ahead to spruce up my backyard.

As lunchtime rolled around on the appointed day, I rushed home from work to see how things were going. I stepped through the French doors that overlook the pool area and was amazed at what I saw: The landscaping was all planted and looking beautiful, but the sight of Tony sitting on the edge of the pool in just his birthday suit, his right fist wrapped around his cock, was even more beautiful. My knees went weak, and I just about passed out. I had never seen him nude before, not even in the showers at the gym. What a vision!

I stood there and watched for a while as Tony brought himself closer and closer to eruption, his dick getting more and more massive. (Of course, by now I was rock-hard myself and leaking like the *Titanic.*) Tony would run both hands between his thighs, then move one hand across his sculpted abs while pinching a nipple with the other. Then he would rub his armor-plated pecs while stroking his cock with a slow, effortless motion. God, I needed to join in! I needed to be the one doing all that to him.

I decided to give it a shot. By then I was out of my clothes, right hand wrapped around my own cock, so I unlocked the door and stepped outside, standing directly across the pool from Tony. The music from his truck was playing pretty loud, so it took a minute before he spotted me. When he did he didn't move. He didn't run away. He nodded his head and smiled at me. And he kept on doing what he'd been doing.

I dived into the pool and broke the surface positioned perfectly between his legs, within inches of his beautiful uncut cock. He waved his dick back and forth in front of my mouth, and I positioned myself with my tongue out and my lips spread, waiting for him to slide it down my throat. But he just continued to tease me by waving it back and forth, one time even tapping my left cheek with it. I moved to go down on him, but he pushed me back with a stern shake of his head. I begged him to let me suck his cock, but he said he just wanted to shoot his load all over me. Now, I would much rather have had the satisfaction of knowing I helped suck some of that ball juice out of him, but I knew there would be some satisfaction in having this god's juicy load smeared all over me, so I relented and waited in anticipation of what was to come.

Actually, it was very erotic watching from below as he worked himself over, and it was obvious that he was really getting off on being watched. Without any moaning or warning of any kind, the first spurt shot out with incredible force and splatted against my right cheek. The second went mostly up my right nostril, but I positioned myself to catch some of it in my mouth. The rest splashed down on my chest and shoulder. When he finished, I rubbed his come off my face with my fingers and sucked each finger dry.

Tony lay back beside the pool and thanked me for helping him get off. I in turn thanked him for landscaping my backyard. I think I got the better of the deal.

M.R., Tampa, Fla.

A Long, Slow Cruise

During the summer of 1980, I met a sailor from the USSR in a bar in London. He was 28 years old, extremely attractive, about 5 foot 9, chunky, and dark-haired. He'd never been outside the Soviet Union. His English was so bad that I had great difficulty understanding him. After I got him to share my table, it was quite interesting to "talk" to him in sign language. He got quite drunk and seemed lonely. It slipped out that he was a married man, but it seemed to me he was so drunk and horny, it didn't matter whether he was picking up a man or a women. So when he asked me up to his room for a chat and drinks, I jumped at the offer.

He took a cold shower to sober up. When he came out of the bathroom, he was wearing only a towel around his waist. He walked right over to me and started to kiss me.

There wasn't much foreplay, and he seemed totally uninterested in oral sex. All he wanted to do was fuck me.

I was already horny as hell, even before seeing that Russian guy's cock stiffening and getting longer by the minute! It was eight or nine inches long but only about 1½ inches in diameter.

After applying some K-Y, he started to enter me. His cock moved smoothly; it glided in. It seemed to take an incredibly long time for him to finally get all the way in and for me to feel the roughness of his pubic hair pressing against my fuck hole. The sheer pleasure of being fucked by this long, probing cock sent shivers through my whole body. I was able to enjoy the penetrating strokes without feeling the pain of being stretched too much. I felt as if the cock was reaching new parts of me. He seemed to be the type that performed in slow motion. I was feeling wild, and his continual slow movements made me feel even more crazed. I urged him to go faster, but no way. He was taking his time, building up the sexual tension, and I was biting him to ease the intensity.

When he was ready to come, I had already been on the threshold for what seemed like an eternity. Only then did he speed up, and we both came together. The climax was powerful indeed.

We had sex again that night, but I was so sleepy that I was still half asleep when he fucked me. I just let him do it for his own sexual satisfaction. Next morning the sex act was different. This time both of us enjoyed the slow and sensual approach. There was no urgency (at least for me) like the first time. I just lay back and enjoyed the blissfulness of being penetrated gently and massaged internally by his cock. When we came, it was a quiet, gentle satisfaction totally unlike the sweaty, frantic coupling and climax of the night before.

K.P., Singapore

◆ Love Ain't Just for Tennis ◆

The other day my buddy comes over and says he's going to play some tennis and do I wanna come too? Well, no way did I want to play tennis. I hate sports—always have—especially sissy sports. If I gotta play something, at least I want it to be a man's sport, like football or something.

Anyway, my buddy there says he needs me to come 'cause they're playing doubles and they only got three people. I ain't held a tennis racket in my hand since high school. But I figure if it'll help out a friend, then he'll owe me one, and I happen to know that he gives great head, so I figure it's like an investment. So I go.

As soon as I see the other guys, I know why my buddy all of the sudden took up tennis. They're hot and hung; I can see that right away.

Those prissy little tennis whites they got on don't fool me. These are working men; I can tell from their muscles and the way they stand around, trying to look like they got more money than they do.

One of 'em is real beefy-looking. He's tall, probably 6 foot 3, maybe 4.

He's got tanned skin, like maybe he's been working in construction or something. He looks great with those white clothes on. His legs are like tree trunks, and he's really hairy, like a huge bear.

The other one looks more like a sportsman than anyone out there on the court. He's a lot shorter, about 5 foot 8. His sandy blond hair is short, and it makes him look like a university student: a good kid, someone who don't get into trouble very often. I wondered if he'd ever had the dick slipped to him.

Well, we started the game on time, which is a good thing, because I couldn't stand those polyester shorts they made me wear. I'd just as soon have worn some Levi's cutoffs, but when I run and jump around with those things on, my dick just goes floppin' right outa place. I was afraid I'd scare some housewife or something, so I left 'em home.

After about half an hour of playing, I started to sweat up a storm. My shirt was all soaked, and I could feel the juices in my crotch too. At first it was hard to tell if it was the 90-degree heat or the hunky bodies on the other side of the net, but pretty soon I knew what was getting me hot, and it wasn't no damn tennis ball.

We broke the game up around noon because the courts started to get crowded and we were getting tired. I pretended like I could go on forever. I didn't want these guys to think I was a pussy, but I was glad when they stopped. Someone suggested a cool shower in the locker room, and my ears—and something else—pricked right up.

All the way in, we laughed and joked like a bunch of buddies. The tall one with the tan took a slap at my ass as we walked into the showers, but I brushed it off as a macho gesture. Secretly I wanted to drop to my knees and take a bite outa his ass.

We headed right for the showers. My buddy—the guy I arrived with—took the last stall, and the short blond guy followed. That left me and the George Hamilton knockoff all alone.

At first I went on with my shower—business as usual. I tried not to notice that this guy was standing right next to me, but every time that gigantic sausage of his swung back and forth, my mouth just about dropped open. I licked my lips and started to salivate, just thinking about satisfying my hunger on a piece of meat like that.

Then, before I know what the hell is going on, this guy takes a grab at my cock. Granted, it's nowhere near as big as his is, but it's a pretty decent tool. I guess he thought so too, because the next thing I know, he's down on his knees, sucking on my rod like a fucking vacuum. I never woulda guessed I'd get a blow job like that when I hit the courts, but I figured maybe there was something to this tennis game after all.

I leaned back against the wet tiles and watched him as he snaked up and down my shaft, slurping at the cool water and letting it dribble into and out of his mouth. He worked my cock like a pro, squeezing and applying pressure just where I liked it.

I'd been sucked by tons of women in my day, but I tell you, I've never found one who could even come close to a dude when it comes to oral sex. Only a guy knows what it feels like and only a guy can get you off like that.

So this one keeps on sucking and ramming my cock down his throat until my pubes are up his fucking nose. But he don't stop, and he don't gag even a little bit. He just takes it again and again, harder and harder. He's determined to suck my goddamned brains out.

Now I'm getting close. My feet dig into the floor, and I grab on to his head for support. He draws his cheeks in and sucks as hard as he can, and I end up shooting all over his face. But he don't even slow down to notice.

He puts his big tanned hands on my hips and flips me around, pushing my face into the wall. I grab the tile and hold on 'cause I don't know what the hell he's doing.

Well, it don't take him long to make his point, 'cause the next thing I know, that huge prod of his is shoving its way up my asshole. He don't even give me time to relax before he pops my hole. And it slides in like nobody's business.

He's grunting behind me like some kinda animal, and every now and then he takes a bite out of my shoulder. I can't stop him, and I wonder if he knows what he's doing. Anybody could walk by at any time, and I start to get a little nervous.

But he just keeps plugging that massive tool up into my guts without even stopping to catch his breath. His thrusts are pushing me up against the wall, and before I can get the rhythm down and really start enjoyin' it, he comes all over my insides.

Then he plops out, rinses off, and he's gone.

I'm still in a daze, right? I don't know what the fuck is happening. So I just finish my shower and try to track down my buddy, hoping he ain't left without me 'cause I don't wanna walk home.

I find him in the lobby, sitting there with a shit-eating grin all over his face. He says how'd I like it, and I tell him, "Fine." Then he tells me that he don't owe me nothing anymore, and when I say, "How come?" he says that he's already made sure I was paid up. That's when I knew that he sent that guy in there after me.

Not a bad deal, all in all. I help a friend out, and he helps me out. Sure as hell beats a six-pack.

A.T., Seal Beach, Calif.

◆ Married Men ◆

Since I was 18, I have had sex with a good many married men. Usually they have come on to me in straight bars, gay bars, hotel lobbies, airport terminals, department stores, restaurants, and parks. And, of course, in men's rooms everywhere. Some were actually gay but married, some were bi, and some were straight, wanting to find out what it would be like to have sex with another male stud. Each and every time the studs have enjoyed our sex together—except for one. He loved having me suck his cock, and he loved fucking my ass. He said it was hotter and tighter than any cunt he had had! He even enjoyed sucking my cock and swallowing my come, but he wouldn't let me fuck his ass. He said he couldn't handle it: "Too fucking big!" His loss!

On one memorable occasion I was picked up in a straight

bar in San Diego by a young married couple, both in their late 20s. She was a good-looking dark-haired gal with a nice trim figure. The husband was a real hunk. Six feet, about 180 pounds of solid suntanned muscle. He had light brown hair, a mustache, and a smile that wouldn't quit. They asked me to sit at their table, and during our conversation, which had gotten around to the subject of sex, I admitted to them that I was gay. When they heard that they smiled at each other, and the wife asked if I would go with them to their house and have sex with her husband while she watched. I looked at him, wondering what he was going to say about this. He said they both wanted to find some male for him to have sex with because on many occasions they had shared a female and now they wanted a male. So we ended up going to their house.

We no sooner got there than we were in the bedroom, all three of us stark naked. The wife relaxed on a chaise lounge, playing with herself, while her stud husband and I sucked and fucked each other for almost four hours. I have always enjoyed being watched by others while having sex with another stud, but that time, being watched by the stud's wife, was a fantastic turn-on! He also got completely into it, sucking my cock and letting me fuck his tight ass. He especially enjoyed fucking my ass. In fact, when he fucked my ass, he told his wife that it felt as tight and as hot as her pussy.

I got $250 and an invitation to return. The husband said he would look forward to our getting together again. We did several more times. Each time, the wife watched.

Married studs can be great sex. I still maintain contact

with a few married studs, and when we get together it's always hot! I guess some people would be surprised as hell if they knew how many married studs want and need male-male sex. I am a part-time stripper for private parties, and when I perform for a straight audience of married couples, I can see those married studs getting hard-ons, fondling and rubbing their cocks while watching me do my stuff, much to the howling delight of their wives. I'm sure many, if not all, of those married studs fantasize about what it might be like to have sex with me. I always try my best to let them know what I have to offer, because I always strip down to a string pouch, and if I have a really hot and receptive audience, I tear off the pouch just before I leave the stage or floor and give them a look at what I really have to offer. And as I do, my package elicits more than a few appreciative gasps. Of course, I have received many offers as a result, many of them from married men. Guess that's why they call me Stud!

F.C., Oak Harbor, Wash.

◆ My Own Private Dick ◆

By profession I'm an English teacher. But part of me has always fancied myself to be a writer. I contribute articles now and then to a few of the smaller gay papers here in the New York area. It doesn't pay, but it's a real kick to see my name—and my writing—in print.

I knew that the whole writing thing was really worth it when I finally got the chance to interview my favorite TV star. He played an ex-CIA agent turned sort of private eye. The show was sometimes written like a comic book, but they could have spoken pig latin for all I cared. I tuned in just to watch him.

Now, I knew this dude wasn't gay, but I still wanted to interview him for my paper. Normally they wouldn't have accepted the story, but my editor is a good friend of mine. He knew that I just wanted to get into this guy's pants—or as close as I could get. He told me that if I could find a gay angle to the story, he'd print it.

While I was riding up in the hotel elevator, I couldn't help grinning to myself as I wondered if he was really "bigger than life."

He looked fantastic when he opened the door. Oh, maybe a little ragged around the eyes, but other than that, he could have passed for a guy half his age.

From his bio I knew that he was 42 (I've always had a thing for older men) and unmarried. He made his home in Manhattan during the shooting season, and he also had a little beach house in Northern California.

His short, hefty frame was dressed casually in baggy blue jeans and a well-worn T-shirt. He invited me in immediately and tried to make me as comfortable as possible.

It wasn't easy, I'll tell you. With his sitting so near to me, it was all I could do to keep from showing my boner. I kept squirming in my seat like I had to pee, and a couple of times I even got up and paced the room, pretending to admire the view over the park.

I don't know if it was the wet spot on my pants or what, but before I knew it, he was sitting dangerously close to me and making innuendos like crazy.

I was really kind of surprised at first, and I wondered if my intentions were really that obvious. Besides, he had to be careful; did he really want to risk his career on a few minutes alone with my dong?

Hardly. It never really got past the innuendo with him, but an interesting thing happened before I left.

I couldn't stand the buildup in my cock anymore, so I excused myself and went to the bathroom. I groaned as I stood in front of the mirror and eyed my sausage bulging through my pants. I knew that he'd seen it, and I felt like a stupid ass.

I pulled my dick out to take a piss, but it would hardly let me touch it. It was aching and raring to go—and more than a little disappointed that there was no action to be had. So we did the next best thing.

I grabbed it by the loose foreskin near the balls and squeezed gently. I could feel the blood rushing up to the head, and soon it was rock-hard and completely erect.

Thoughts of my TV hero in the next room filled my head as I stroked my meat. I fantasized about him watching me through the keyhole and wiggled my ass back and forth for his benefit.

I imagined it was his hands on my throbbing dick as little drops of goo formed on the slit and dripped down all over my fingers.

Closing my eyes and getting completely into my fantasy, I reached up under my shirt and began to tweak my nipples. Each flip of my finger brought me closer and closer.

I massaged my left pec hard and kneaded the flesh near my armpit. Bringing my attention back to my dong, I yanked my hand out of my shirt and grabbed my dick with both hands. One tugged gently on the balls, bringing them down farther and farther to keep myself from shooting right away. The other worked my veiny shaft, slipping across its surface back and forth.

I breathed heavily and heaved forward. Then I knew I couldn't control myself any longer. I bent forward and closed my eyes. My whole body racked with spasms as I let loose a torrent of hot, rich come into the toilet bowl. Some splattered on the wall, and, after considering it for a moment, I decided to leave it as a token of my appreciation.

I didn't want to leave the john right away because my face and chest were all splotchy. He'd know in a second that I had just beaten off. I killed a few more minutes by washing my face and straightening my tie. I winked at myself in the mirror and headed out to conclude the interview.

When I opened the door, I was shocked to see my TV idol lying on the couch, facing away from me. I tiptoed up behind him so he wouldn't hear me; I thought maybe he was asleep.

His shirt was pulled out of his pants, and his clothes looked in disarray. His legs were splayed over the back of the couch, and it looked like he was just dozing off. Then I saw the red splotches down the side of his neck.

He'd been jerking off too.

That's as close as I ever got to realizing my fantasy with him, but it's nice to think that he was fantasizing about me while I was dreaming of him. I think about it all the time now, especially when I'm jerking off.

M.B., Long Island, N.Y.

◆ Ned's Story ◆

The war in Vietnam was nearly over by 1973 for most American forces as well as members of the antiwar movement. Having been at different times both a military employee and an SDS member, I often felt the pull of divided loyalties, sometimes personally. I was a bit of an Army brat, by way of Fort Hamilton and the Brooklyn Naval Yard. I had met Ned at a downtown bar frequented by air base personnel stationed at Plattsburgh, New York. I was a full-time truck driver for my father, who'd had a heart attack, and a part-time bouncer at another local townie-college bar, so I was kept busy after college and forced to delay going to graduate school. I met Ned's current ex-wife (he always seemed to be between marriages) while drinking one night, a habitual preoccupation of mine at the time. I considered it as my night job.

I was probably the only openly gay person in Plattsburgh then. As a bouncer I was known more for being able to take punches than to give them. Other employees or friends constantly rescued my sweet little ass. Being slightly notorious, on a small-town level, I got to know lots of people from questioning bar patrons—and those wanting to question me. Ned's ex-wife was one of the latter. She considered Ned a son of a bitch. Even though he was drunk, I fell in love with him at first sight; I still remember those grey-green eyes under that soft thatch of sandy hair. His hair, eyes, and mustache remind me now of Rick Donovan, the porn star, and the two have become almost twins in my memory, especially when it comes to size.

Our first sex happened that same night—or rather the next morning. He had no car or driver's license. He'd done a tour in 'Nam as a Marine and then reenlisted in the Air Force as a medic and lived on base. He was always on report or up on charges, which left him with little real choice for catching a ride except from his current wife or his buddies in the barracks. For a military base, security was pretty lax, and the SPs let us through with a wave after Ned explained I was only driving him back to barracks and returning. Ned had duty call in three hours, but we still had to beware of his barracks mates, some of whom would have reported us. After all, I wasn't supposed to be there—much less doing what we were doing. That first time seemed to start from the very moment the door closed, as we kissed passionately and pulled our shirts off, opening our pants and falling onto his bed. His hand quickly went over my mouth, between our heated lips.

"Quiet!" he whispered. "Or they'll hear us, and I'll be on report again."

His hand fell away, and our moist mouths met again, and our sliding hands pulled both pants and underwear farther down but not off. We had to be prepared to dress and be in separate bunks if the security patrol knocked. The twisted sense of urgency made our hardened dicks explode with come in almost no time at all. My loud cries were muffled by his mouth locked tightly over mine as our thrusting hips ground into each other with wild spasms. Although it was over quickly, we seemed unable to stop ourselves and went on and rolled onto the floor, where carpet burns would occasionally halt our efforts as we continuously shot again and again. Suddenly the short, sharp knock of the duty officer rattled the door.

"Duty call—0700," the voice rasped.

"Ready for call," Ned answered quickly while we pulled up our pants and donned our shirts as rapidly as possible. I slipped out the rear barracks exit while Ned went through the front entrance and hopped into the car outside. I drove him to duty at the hospital unit. As we left the base without being challenged, I promised myself that this was not the last night!

Four nights later I drove back to the hospital on the outside edge of the base looking for Ned. I had called the barracks earlier and gotten his duty station, so I knew where to find him, having worked there myself as a civilian driver. The other orderly on duty smiled and directed me to one of the triage rooms on the side hallway, where Ned lay asleep, snoring gently on a hospital gurney bed. I crept up beside him and touched his lips with the tip of my tongue, driving it slowly into his mouth, running my hand over his chest and deep into the crotch of his pants, sliding onto and grabbing his swiftly hardening dick. He turned onto his side on the gurney, and his hand slid my zipper down and turned my dick around and yanked it out of my pants. We both were soon hard and dripping come all over ourselves and the gurney. Once again our groaning voices were muffled by our mouths' being locked together, and our bodies arched as we simultaneously shot our loads, which slicked our bared chests and dripped from the steel bars of the gurney onto the tiled hospital floor. Again we had to recover as rapidly as possible when we heard the other orderly's footsteps coming down the hall.

"Ned, it's your turn for desk duty!" he called.

"Yeah, OK," Ned answered slowly. "I'll be right there." Looking at me, he added, "You have to leave now." He rose and, holding my hips, kissed me deeply. I lost myself in the melding of our mustaches, now slippery with our sweaty sex. As my knees steadied and our labored breathing eased, we cleaned ourselves up as well as the gurney and went out to the duty desk, where I left him and the other orderly, who grinned again as we separated.

By the second month we were a pretty steady item, but we still had to be wary. One barracks mate across the hall got jealous, while a cute blond who shared Ned's bathroom got pissed after I up-chucked all over the toilet one raucous night. It was touch-and-go back in town too, as his ex-wife started telling more than she knew, but we had also provoked her in public once or twice.

Getting high or stoned was also part of those 'Nam-college years, and the local hippie population was a part of my social fabric as well as that of the town's. Ned and I were invited to a friend's parents' house on the cliffs of Cumberland Head overlooking Lake Champlain. After exchanging social pleasantries, we shared a few joints. Eventually we took a canoe out onto the lake. We were soon soaking wet from all the paddle splashing and canoe rocking as we headed across the dark green waves; we were so stoned, we even laid our dicks across the metal slats, which quickly stiffened in the breeze. After we returned to dock, Ned headed us back up the cliff toward the house. Halfway there he pulled me down into a pup tent that was set up in the backyard, and we proceeded to make out on its grassy floor. We were soon all sliding bodies and turgid dicks, wrapping our legs around each other, one's toes digging into the other's soles. The nearby laughter and noise of our friends embarrassed us, and we fled to my car and headed back to my apartment, dressed only in towels.

The drive back was dangerous enough as I tried to keep one hand on the steering wheel while the other half held, half resisted his groping of my crotch as we drove through the center of town in broad daylight. Luckily, there were no cops around. Once in the apartment, we threw our towels and clothes off and grappled again. But this time Ned's mouth moved from my lips down my sweating chest to my waiting stiff cock. Those wet licks over my dick head and down its shaft gave me the shivers, and I grabbed his head, running my fingers through his hair in ecstatic anticipation. It wasn't even close to being my first experience with oral sex, but the sight of his doelike eyes peering over my leaking shaft sent me into paroxysms of orgasm. Ned swallowed as much of my spend seed as he could, his hands cupping my balls and forcing my dick farther down his throat. He then pulled his lips slowly off my still-stiff cock and, grinning, asked, "Was that worth the drive?"

I nodded my head weakly and drew him toward me. "I think I'll remember it for the rest of my life," I replied softly, not knowing how prophetic that was to be.

As I began to kiss him and return the favor, he stopped me and said heavily, "I have to go. I can't miss duty call again, or I'll be on report for the month."

Then he ducked into the shower, and after he dried off and dressed I drove him back to the hospital in time for his duty. That was the next-to-last time we would be together that summer. In July, as I prepared to move to North Carolina in order to restart my graduate work, I asked Ned to join me once his tour of duty was finished. It was a typical, tearful farewell done country-style in a white pickup on a side street at sunset. It did neither of us any good. Ned was not the kind of man to be led around.

Two years later I drove north to see my family and, of course, Ned. I had let his memory become part of my life story—my 'Nam-college-USO time. Twenty years later it still lingers like slow discoveries of forgotten details even as I write about it. I had maintained a correspondence with Ned in between his discharges and admissions to veterans' hospitals, jails, and various treatment programs for what is now known as PTSD (post-traumatic stress disorder), which I had been blind to during our time together.

I drove up to Indian Lake, where Ned had built a cabin behind his mother's house. That passionate fire in his clouded emerald eyes still held me, and we never did make it through a second round of beers. The lust that had arced across the telephone wires during earlier phone calls was enough to have us unclothed and on the bed in seconds. We engaged in a fast flurry of moving hands and lips, becoming a rapid sixty-nine that seemed to blur into hot hands, moist mouths, and grunting groans. The result was an ongoing orgasm that sparked some hidden core within me. Up until that point I hadn't been very sexually versatile (more top than bottom), but someone in North Carolina had broadened my horizons—as well as other areas. I pulled Ned up over my crotch and felt the full length of his cock burning into my shocked skin.

"Where's your lube?" I asked, and from over the bed he pulled out a green tube of U.S. Army petroleum jelly.

"This isn't going to be easy for me, so do it the way I want, OK?" I half begged.

His hands cradled my head as he kissed my eyes and whispered softly in my ears: "Give it to me any way you want. I'll be careful. Just tell me what to do, OK?"

I worked my fingers vigorously up my asshole, liberally covered his hard behemoth with the slick lubricant, and lay on my back with my ass on the edge of the bed. Lifting my legs up on his shoulders, I slowly started to pull him into me. Having been fucked before was of little help in dealing with this monster cock. My years of martial arts breathing exercises helped control the pain as I felt my rectum being wrenched. Twice it was necessary to relube his engorged dick head. When his throbbing piston finally dove into and stretched apart my sphincter, I could feel a warm, glowing, almost electric sensation that began at the base of my spine and grew deeper and warmer as Ned's long cock plunged into me over and over again. My own dick started to harden again and expanded between us as Ned rolled his stomach muscles against it. At that instant our eyes locked, and, lost in the total sensuality of the moment, we recognized a special bond that I guess I'd always known but had just forgotten. We'd found it at the same time.

Physical sensations shocked my body into orgasm as the heat in Ned's groin ground into my balls. I swear I felt his come pelting deep into my gut. I know I felt the pulsating waves of expansion and contraction with each new thrust of his rod into and over my insides. Luckily, we were far enough in the woods not to be heard. Ned's cry was long and piercing, and we shuddered together as we simultaneously pumped our cream.

"Man, let's try that again!" he said, looking down at his cock, which, while no longer hard, was still enormous.

"When my ass recovers, I'll let you know," I gasped as I wiped up and headed for the bathroom. I sat on the makeshift commode and looked at him.

"It's never been like that," I stammered. "I mean... You know...believe me! That was *so* good. I mean, it always was good, but this was...*incredible!* It's got to mean something—the way I felt."

"No! Stop it! This is going to be just like the last time, and I'm not leaving!" he stated flatly and started to throw on his clothes. I felt as if I were shitting out my heart, not still-warm come and blood. I looked across the room and knew I'd gone too far—again.

"I know you won't come to stay, but always remember it as place to escape to when you need to hide out," I said slowly.

"I knew that already," he replied, gazing at me. "But I get my benefits here, so I stay."

We kissed our last kiss almost 20 years ago, and as he left for the trail to his house and I for the one to my car, our eyes met in a look that would always say, "I am here now, completely, and that's the only way there is, and the only way to remember it is once, completely."

This I have done.

R.S., New York, N.Y.

◆ Paradise Regained ◆

The phone rang, jarring me into consciousness. I fumbled for it in the dark, barely able to read the numbers of the clock. It said 2:15. *Damn,* I thought as I grabbed the receiver, *I hate calls in the middle of the night. They're either bad news or a wrong number.*

"Hello," I mumbled.

"Charles, I need to come and see you tomorrow. My plane gets in at 11:30 in the morning, Flight 735. If you can't meet me, I'll take a cab."

"I'll meet you."

That was all. I lay there, and the memories washed over me. It had been 35 years since I had heard Jake's voice, but he didn't need to tell me who he was. I would never forget.

The war was winding down in the Pacific. I had finished naval ROTC and received orders to report to a landing craft in the waters off the Philippines. When I finally arrived aboard ship, I found that my quarters were a cubbyhole I shared with Jake.

He was not too happy to share the meager space, but we soon became friends. There were five of us officers, all ensigns except the captain. It wasn't long before I discovered the routines and took my share of duty. Nor was it long before I started having stirrings in my groin over Jake.

Jake was as macho as they come. A picture of the beautiful woman he had married two weeks before shipping out was tacked on the bulkhead. He talked about her all the time. Like everyone but me, he had a deep tan. He worked out on a contraption he had built in the forward chain locker, and it showed.

I found myself preoccupied with watching him, especially in our own quarters when he had stripped to his shorts. Every time I see those old war movies, I am reminded of those baggy boxer shorts; that was all we wore in our quarters. We even slept in them; a sheet was too much cover in those hot, stuffy confines.

When Jake went to the head to shower, I often went and sat on the crapper just to be near him. There was only half a shower curtain, and I was so close that sometimes I got sprayed, but the view was breathtaking. His cock was long, even when relaxed. His balls looked small because the scrotum swung so low. His belly was hard, and his pecs, superb. The lines down his back and around the curves of his butt reminded me of Michelangelo's *David*. Watching him lathering up was a voyeur's dream.

The weeks turned into months, and the war in Europe

ended, but our friendship grew. He slept in the bunk below me, and sometimes at night I could feel him jacking off, shaking the entire bed. I wanted to kid him about it, but I didn't dare. One night when he came in from watch, I became aware that his face was close to mine in the darkness; I could feel his breath. Then he touched my arm gently, a caress.

I stopped breathing. His hand lingered for minutes before he withdrew it and stretched out on his own bunk. Then the familiar vibrations began.

After that night, whenever he got off duty in the middle of the night, he would stand there in the dark beside our bunk, and I would feel his hand moving up and down my body. It always produced a boner, but he never touched my dick. I had no idea what was going on. To say that I was a virgin would have been a vast understatement—I was a novice. I was naive.

I had been attracted to men for as long as I could remember, but nothing had ever happened. This, you'll remember, was before anything was available to read; no one talked about homosexuality.

For years I thought I was the only deviate in the world. I had joined the Navy not so much in an effort to fulfill some hot gay fantasy but because I thought that there I could become a man and forget all those dreadful imaginings that haunted me.

Yet night after night, Jake caressed me. Then one night his lips touched my cheek. I threw my arm around him and pulled him to me. He broke away and got into his bunk.

In the morning he said nothing, and I knew of nothing to

say. For a week after that, he'd come in, pull off his clothes, and lie down without touching me. I couldn't stand the isolation. So one night, when I heard him coming down the corridor, I climbed down from my bunk and lay in his, just waiting.

I heard the usual sounds as he hung up his uniform; I felt the bed sagging as he sat down and took off his shoes. I felt him jumping in surprise when he touched me, but he did not pull away. He stretched out and took me in his arms. We kissed deep and long. We explored each other's body with lips and fingers.

We pressed our aching cocks together. When he finally did touch me, I exploded immediately. I circled his dick with my hand, and as soon as I started to jack him off, he came too. It was more wonderful than I could have possibly imagined.

After the war ended, he went home to his wife, and I went to college and eventually on to San Francisco. I lived a good life from then on, but I never forgot Jake. And then he called me.

I went into town the next day to meet him at the airport. I didn't recognize him until he was right in front of me. He grinned and looked more like the Jake I remembered.

Driving into the city, he poured out his story. He had gone to a tearoom at Memorial Park, as was his custom. At the urinal beside him was a hunky brunet with a handsome boner. When Jake reached over to touch it, the man pulled out a badge. Two other plainclothes officers appeared, and Jake was handcuffed and taken to jail. The next day his name, along with 17 others, was printed in the paper.

His marriage had disintegrated, and he lost his job. Now he had come to me.

I put his stuff in the guest room, and the next morning he started looking for a job. Because of his age, he found few places that even wanted to talk to him. Each night we found lots to catch up on, and then we would retire to our separate beds. He seemed to be too discouraged for sexual feelings, but I found that they were growing in me.

Sometime in the middle of the fourth night, I stole into his room. Through the soft light from the window, I could see him clearly. His hair was gray—even grayer than mine—but his thin face was still quite handsome. I stood there, stroking myself into arousal, and after many minutes I slid into bed beside him and wrapped him in my arms.

Sex was slow and delicious. If I closed my eyes, I could imagine those nights aboard ship, but the present sight was better. He had stayed in better shape than I had, but that made little difference. I reveled in his hairy chest. I buried my face in his crotch, taking in the man smell of him, feeling the sharp, scratchy hair against my cheek. His cock was as magnificent as I remembered, though the sac had shrunk somewhat through the years. His come was sweet.

When I had drained his juice, he slid down in the bed and made love to me. He teased me with his tongue, sliding up and down my cock as if it were a Popsicle. I stood beside the bed, and he knelt before me while I fucked his face. After I flooded his mouth with come, we fell into bed and slept until the morning sun roused us. I didn't go to work that day—or the next.

Shortly after, Jake went to work in my shop. He also

moved his things into my room. Tonight we celebrate our tenth anniversary, or our 45th—depending on when you start counting. We have no plans for the celebration—at least, none that involve anyone else. We'll probably go to bed early!

K.W., Colorado Springs, Colo.

◆ Pigs in a Blanket ◆

I knew Officer S. Doogan from the time we were both sitting in the back of a criminal justice class. "Doog," as I used to call him, was pretty laid back, like me, so we got along from the start. We'd go out for beers after school, and I learned that he was married, had a kid, drove a motorcycle, loved baseball, and played softball on a team in his town's weekend league. He'd worked as a lifeguard, even served time in the Navy, so when I tell you that nothing about him remotely hinted of cocksucker, you gotta believe me.

Truth was, I was 21 when I met him. Doog was five years my senior. I guess every guy around my age wonders what it would be like—you know—to do it with another guy. It's not like you're in a locker room with a whole team of your buddies and suddenly you turn into a man-loving slut. But late at night, when I was awakened up by a hard-on, I'll admit I started thinking of Doog while lubing my fat eight-incher with spit, stroking just the top inch and the head, growling his name into the pillow as I blew a few hot strings of come across my chest.

Doog was a real handsome fucker, for sure. He stood about 6-foot-3 and kept his hair—silvered just above the ears—short on the sides, flat on the top. He had dark blue eyes and for a while wore a neat mustache on his handsome face. He wore sneakers and blue jeans, polo shirts and sunglasses most of the time, except for weekends, when he hung out in sweat socks, stirrup pants, cleats, and ball caps. But in 1992, the year I decided to pursue pre-law, Doog started dressing differently. The last time I saw him before his divorce, he was decked out in his police uniform, looking like a million bucks in his black button-down dress shirt and tie, uniform pants, black boots, policeman's hat, and gold shield. He told me he was aiming for the motorcycle patrol beat. From that point on, I stopped feeling guilty about beating off over him.

Like I said, me and Doog, you'd never think either of us was into dick. He once told me that he'd fucked his ex-wife after a police function on his motorcycle in full view of the security cameras just so his buddies would know he was the *man.* And me—I'd had plenty of pussy myself since the start of college. But the day I saw Doog standing tall and proud in his pressed black cop duds, I knew coochie would never be enough for me. I'd really fallen for him. Fallen hard. But not nearly as hard as Doog fell the following summer.

We hadn't seen much of each other for ten months. I had school, he, second shift. It was a Friday afternoon, real ball-busting 80-degree weather with humidity. I was driving with the roof down and my shirt off when I caught sight of flashing blue lights in the rearview mirror, followed by the blast of a motorcycle cop's siren. I had just pulled out my driver's license when I heard a deep, familiar voice grumble, "Put that away!"

I peeled off my shades to see my surprised face reflected in another set of silver sunglasses under the motorcycle helmet. It was Doog. He'd shaved his 'stache, but his smile caused the heat already making me sweat gallons to burn even hotter.

"Doog!" I exclaimed.

"I saw you down near Main Street," he said, putting a hand on my bare, tanned shoulder. I tried not to react to the strong squeeze of his leather-gloved fingers, but Doog's touch, like the smell of his breath and all that police leather, was like a punch to my gut.

I patted Doog's hand and smiled. "How ya doin', buddy?"

Doog didn't answer right away. Instead, he tipped his head, motorcycle helmet and all, at an angle, even though his sunglasses were already shielding his eyes. "Not good, man. Not so good."

Now it was my turn. I slapped the hard-packed gut above Doog's gun belt. "What do you mean?"

"Going through the big D, man," he answered. "I moved out. Got an apartment. It kinda sucks."

"Why didn't you call me?" I growled.

"I wouldn't dump my shit on you."

"You couldn't. We're *pals,* remember?"

Doog grinned. The inside of my car got even hotter. "I could use a pal." Pulling out his pad and pen, Doog scribbled down his new number. "I'm off Sunday. Maybe we could get together. Play cards. Watch the game. Down a few cold ones."

Taking the paper, I saluted. "Yes, sir, Officer."

I drove off, but for the next two days I found myself bumping into walls, popping hard-ons at the thought of him, and counting down the hours till I'd be with him again.

Doog's new place was in a brick apartment building. It wasn't much of a home—first floor, one bedroom—but it had air-conditioning. He buzzed me in, and I walked down the barely lit hallway carrying a six-pack.

He answered the door in an old T-shirt, ball cap, and navy cotton jogging shorts, no socks. "Hey, man!"

I gave Doog a manly hug. His closeness, despite the welcome chill from the air-conditioning, caused the sweat already making my pits and crotch damp to flow even more. Doog smelled good, like soap and clean, masculine skin, no cologne. He hugged me hard. Over his shoulder I caught a sight of his motorcycle patrol uniform slung over the single chair at his kitchen table. The door to the bedroom was open. It was full of cardboard boxes, no bed. He would later tell me she'd gotten that, the reason for the futon covered in blankets in the living room. The TV and VCR were propped up on a milk crate.

"Sorry about the accommodations," he said. We cracked open two cold ones, then plunked down, ass to ass, on the futon and bedsheets. Doog shifted his left thigh against mine. I wasn't complaining as he flipped on the game. Home team was up, 3–love.

I shook my head. "OK, bro, so what happened?"

"You know," he sighed, slugging down beer. *"Shit."*

"Happens to all of us," I said. "Don't sweat it, Doog."

I hadn't meant to, but I clapped my free hand onto my cop buddy's bare, hairy knee. The prickly, rough hairs at the tips of my fingers had an unexpected effect. In the tight-packed front of my jeans, my dick started to toughen up. Nervously I let go of Doog's knee and took a heavy gulp of cold brew in an attempt to choke down the sudden knowledge of heat in my throat.

"Chicks suck," I said, trying to sound confident. I sent Doog a smile, hoping it would look cocky and cool, but when I glanced up, his intense blue eyes were locked on mine. I watched his unshaven throat puff under the influence of a big swallow.

"They're not like another guy," he growled. "Not like a good buddy."

"I'll drink to that," I stammered, raising my beer.

"I thought you would, pal," Doog said, but instead of toasting me with his beer bottle, he reached over and groped the bulge in my jeans, squeezing it with his big hand.

"What the...?" I think I gasped, dropping the empty bottle. A second later Doog's hairy mouth clamped down on mine. I don't know how long it took for me to untense, to kiss back at the unshaven, rough, beer-tasting lips. By the time Doog's tongue slipped into my open mouth, he'd hauled down my zipper and pulled down my boxers and

was sliding a thumb up and down my knob while gripping the shaft like it was his billy club.

"*Shit,* man!" I huffed when Doog came up for air. I looked deep into his handsome blues, studied the excited, sexy grin on his face, then reached up and fondled the low-hanging tent in his workout shorts. Just as I eased them off his hard-as-nails can, I heard a sharp crack on the TV. Our team had hit another homer. Me, I took Doog's bat in one hand and his two meaty, hairy balls in the other.

"Do it," I heard him order through my confusion. "Suck it good. Suck it like only my best buddy can."

Before I could argue the point, Doog leaned forward, pressing the salty-wet head of his lean, mean seven inches between my lips. I'd always wondered how dick would taste. Doog's was slick and powerful on my tongue. I took him slowly at first, just the head. I'd spent so many nights beating my meat in anticipation of this moment, I didn't want to fuck it up by gagging.

"That's it," Doog moaned. His deep voice urged me on. Soon I had most of him in my mouth, till my nose was buried in the mossy-smelling line of fur around his bat. "Man, I been needing this for a long time!"

I sucked Doog's dick like a greedy cock-slut. But when I tasted something sticky and salty on my tongue, I spit out his cock and licked my lips. It was precome. Yeah, I wanted it. More than anything. Only I didn't want him to shoot too fast.

"This is good, Doog," I whispered, burying my face in his hairy, fat balls. I sniffed at the musky sac before sucking them, one at a time, into my hungry mouth. I even got a taste of that smelly patch behind his nuts where they banged against his ass. It was the dream I'd never expected to come true, but I could smell it, taste it. *It was real.*

Doog whipped off his ball cap and T-shirt, then pulled off mine before ripping the jeans off my butt. I watched, amazed, as he licked my bare toes, all the way to my balls. He then went down on my nuts, even my asshole, eating me out the way we'd both eaten out women. It drove me crazy, the wet, hot feel of his tongue, while the air-conditioning spit cool air over my sweaty, naked body.

Finally Doog took my cock in his mouth and sucked it, as if he'd been doing it for years. I let out a howl. Doog shut me up by feeding me his manhood. We opened the futon up, smoothed out the blankets, and settled into a sixty-nine, each guy chowing on the other, till we both gulped up a flood of nut juice. Doog's was sour and heavy. Real good stuff. Me, I had no trouble drinking it any more than he did mine.

Later that night Doog sat on my face. Doog's butt had lots of short dark hair on it. A perfect ring of black fur surrounded his tight, puckered hole. It was my first taste of real man ass, and as hard to fathom as those first few licks of a guy's hole were, I soon found myself loving it. Doog told me this was his favorite part of sex. *Butt play.* Something his ex-wife and no woman had done for him yet. Doog said he wanted to fuck me after we finished off the six-pack.

"Fuck you," I told him jokingly. "You want to fuck me, you gotta let me fuck *you* first."

To my surprise, he let me.

I mounted Doog doggy-style, and—*fuck*, if he wasn't tighter than any cunt I'd been in before! I must have fucked him for only a few minutes before I shot off again. I stayed inside him but felt something wet running down my balls and legs, cooled by the air conditioner. It wasn't sweat. It was my own come. I pulled out and shoved my tongue between Doog's rock-hard ass cheeks and ate my own tang from his shitter. I licked it off his nuts and hairy legs, where it was dripping, and to get out of being fucked, I swallowed Doog's dick down my throat. All that ass pounding had worked him so close, I got only a few sucks into it when he blasted his motorcycle cop's cream across my tongue. Sucking him off doggy-style made Doog collapse onto the futon, totally spent.

I joined him on the mattress and pulled the covers over us. We lay there the rest of the night, legs and feet and butt cheeks pressed together, hugging each other protectively.

Soon after his divorce was finalized, Doog shipped south for a highway patrol job in Florida. But for the next two months we sucked and fucked almost every night. I eventually gave up my ass to him.

Now, with Doog gone, I realize there are some things that only men can do for me.

And I try to realize it as often as I can.

G.N., Atkinson, N.H.

◆ Rescued From Shore ◆

Every other summer or so, I leave Chicago to go home, to detox from the stress and hassle of the big city. My hometown is small and countrylike, and the pace is comforting. Last summer I met a man and had an experience so out of character from my usual visits that it has stuck with me to this day.

It happened while I was fishing at the lake just outside town. It was a beautiful, sunny morning, and I'd lucked on a secluded cove of my own, somewhat off the road, near a cluster of dusty oaks.

I was fishing from the bank, just getting settled in, when I heard the low rumble of a truck heading in my direction. My irritation at having my secret fishing hole violated gave way when I saw the driver, a strapping god of a man with tousled brown hair, a day's growth of beard and a shining, friendly smile. He gave me a casual wave as he pulled up his rig—a Datsun pickup with a small boat in tow.

"Howdy," he grinned, climbing out and walking toward my spot at the water's edge. "Any luck?"

"Just started," I said. His toned physique, displayed in a tight red T-shirt and skimpy white trunks, featured fuzzy muscular legs, which shimmered in the sun, and a cock that hung loose, ready and lengthy in his shorts. I remember thinking what a pleasure it would be to pull out that prick right then and there and give it a big, wet kiss.

"Yeah, the fishing's supposed to be gettin' real good about this time of year," he said. "But then, you gotta know where to fish." He pointed to the shallows far out into the cove, just outside my casting reach. "Those are where the big ones are."

It was easy for me to agree, for the big fish seemed always to be beyond my reach.

But wait: This man was alone, he had a boat, and he seemed to be hinting for some company.

I was delighted to oblige.

As I helped him ready the boat, he kept up a steady stream of conversation. He seemed pleased to have rescued me from the unproductive shore. He must have done this before, I figured, keeping my eyes on the bulging cords of his biceps.

Well, I was going to make sure that this was one rescue he'd never forget.

I gathered my tackle and readied some other equipment, then helped him get the boat to the water. After a few more preliminaries, we were afloat. The boat scraped in the shallows for the first three feet, stirring up silt and bottom algae, but the strong, swift arms of my friend, whose name turned out to be Justin, maneuvered us expertly out to the open water.

I was sitting in the stern. As I watched him row, I noticed a rise in his shorts: his fat cock, I assumed, brought to life by the friction of his firm, moving thighs.

Justin went on and on, lecturing me on the advantages of working the jigs along the edge of the thickets, a fact I was well acquainted with, but I let him talk—not only because I liked the sound of his cheery, masculine voice but also because it enabled me to stare at him with much less obviousness, and there was a lot of man to look at.

Eventually we rigged our tackle and began to cast along the shoals. Justin was the first to strike. As he landed a frisky, dripping crappie, he gave a victorious whoop and laughed good-heartedly, smacking the fish into one ice chest and reaching into the other for a beer.

"Here!" he said, tossing me a can. "Drink up!" I did and caught a fish shortly thereafter. After that, for every fish we caught, we had another beer, and crappie, by nature, are a very easy fish to catch.

Needless to say, we soon were blitzed. Justin's rowing became erratic, and as the wind picked up, we drifted deep into the thickets, away from the main body of water, till we were hidden behind a veil of reeds and trees.

I had to piss very, very badly. I threw etiquette to the wind, unzipped my pants, pulled out my cock, and let fly.

I felt much better. When I turned back to Justin, he gave me a big smile.

"Good idea," he said, tugging at his own cock.

I watched carefully as he pulled out his prick and, teetering on his knees just inches from my face, pissed over the gunwale. It steamed and bubbled into the water. As he shook the last of it away, his cock began to harden under my captive eye.

It seemed like the natural order of things to reach over and gently stroke it with my free hand, so I did. And then as it swelled and stiffened, I took it in my mouth. There was a moment of surprise—then eager, anxious cooperation.

"Yeah," Justin moaned, "swallow it." He threw down his fishing rod and loosened the rest of his shorts so they fell about his knees, offering unrestricted access to his huge cock, now slipping thickly in and out of my mouth.

The boat continued to bobble in the current and nearly overturned as Justin fell back against the ice chest, pulling my head with him and urging me on. I loved the taste of him and how neatly his cock fit down my throat. I felt as if I couldn't get enough of this hunk, and as I continued to suck delicately along the rims and corridors of his prick, I trailed the fingers of my free hand along the fine hairs of his fat balls.

Justin's moans skipped across the surface of the water.

I could feel his thick come pulsing toward the top of his prick, and as he reached that point, he thrust his strong legs into me to give his cock that extra push. He came then, in great gushing spurts, much more than I was capable of handling, so the excess dribbled out my mouth and down the corners of my chin. His cock still sticky, he withdrew it and smiled.

"Best fuckin' blow job I ever had." He snapped his shorts over the remainder of his hard-on. The bulge it created turned me on so much I wanted to tear his trunks off and start all over again. I think he sensed this because he took a deep breath and gave me a sheepish grin.

"You haven't had enough, have you?" he asked. I obviously hadn't, as I was flushed and hard as a rock, but the boat, buoyed once again by a sharp tail wind, had now eased back into the main channel.

Justin remained lying down against the ice chest, breathing heavily, still high, still hard. A mesh of fishing wire and tackle had him almost tied to the hull, and his cock, like an overheated engine, had just begun to cool.

"Why don't you follow me home?" He smiled lazily.

He must have taken my response for granted; I don't remember. Very shortly we were rowing back toward the shallows and then to the bank. We piled the tackle, fish, and remaining beer in the back of his truck.

"Follow me closely," he commanded, adding, "I live up in the hills."

After passing the east end of the lake, we headed up a wooded road and on to a long, shaded drive.

In his bedroom I watched him unfasten his shorts. His cock shot up into that great hunk of meat I'd been sucking on just an hour ago. "Get undressed," he said, flashing his sexy smile. After I tore my clothes off, he slapped something wet and cold on his cock and drove it home, deep into my ass, a driveshaft of hot steel that probed and melted in my body, with far-reaching, wonderful consequences.

Later we dozed. When I awoke, he had cleaned up, unloaded the truck, filleted the fish, and fried them. All was ready by the time I toddled downstairs, sheepish, sore, and weary from all the excitement.

In the months since then, back at work in the frenzied rat race of Chicago, I've thought of Justin often, and I mark the days on my fisherman's desk calendar until I can again escape, until I can return to my hometown and look up the stranger I met that lucky day at the lake.

J.W., Chicago, Ill.

◆ Ride 'Em, Cowboy ◆

I am 55, and Steve is 44. We live in the same small town in Southern California. I have known and lusted after Steve for more than 25 years.

Steve is a genuine cowboy, complete with handlebar mustache and Stetson. He's 6 foot 2 and 185 pounds of hard, natural muscle, with an obvious basket and a beautiful ass. He is without a doubt the biggest, sexiest womanizer in our little town. He has reached almost folkloric proportions around these parts because of his barroom brawling, cattle rustling, and numerous bastard children. He is, to put it simply, what any red-blooded frontier queer would die for.

Over the years I have attended social functions just to see Steve, to get to know him and have legitimate contact with him. I am unmarried, and the local consensus is that

I'm gay, but since I don't flaunt it and don't molest little children, I am accepted by the local powers that be, and others follow suit.

I work the late-night shift at the city hospital. One recent evening when I came home, my answering machine bore a message—in a muffled, disguised voice—telling me to call a certain number. Puzzled, I did, and the same voice answered. My mysterious caller stated that he needed to talk to me, but he refused to identify himself. After several moments of nonsensical conversation, I bluntly asked if the call had anything to do with my sexual preference. He said it did, and after much cajoling he finally identified himself: It was Steve. I was completely dumbfounded; it was as though God had opened the skies and spoken directly to me!

Steve admitted to being drunk but said he'd had these curious feelings for years. He insisted that he wasn't gay and that he loved his women and children but that he had to satisfy his burning curiosity. He asked if I would please help him. My knees shaking, I said, "Anything! You must have known how I've always felt about you."

Steve then gave me detailed directions to a remote cabin in the woods, telling me he'd leave the porch light on for me. He had his entire first gay-seduction scenario planned out: He would be "asleep," and there would be rubbers and lube on the nightstand. I was to enter the bedroom, strip, and proceed to "fuck him hard"—with no kissing on the mouth—and then leave. When I expressed reservations about coming, he said, "Please, don't make me beg."

My mind was swirling. I initially agreed to go over there,

but after hanging up I thought more about it, and paranoia overcame me. I decided that it must be a hoax or a trap, and I didn't go.

About an hour later I was awakened by my dog's barking. I ventured outside, and standing at the gate was Steve, his head bowed. "Please," he said, "I want to be with you tonight." Well, trap or no trap, I wasn't going to miss this opportunity.

I took his arm and led him inside to the floor in front of the fireplace. He pulled off his sweats and lay down. I began to slowly masturbate him with my hands and mouth, moving down his cock shaft to his drawn-up nuts, then engulfing and eating his ass. As I inserted a finger into his ass, he abruptly shot his load, moaning and writhing around on the floor. He remained hard while I cleaned off his chest, neck, and chin with my tongue, going soft only after I removed my finger from his ass. Steve then dressed and left without a word.

This occurred about a month ago, and I check my answering machine every night now. I am positive he will call again. After all, he never got fucked, and I never got a piece of that hot cowboy ass.

Steve is the third married local "straight" guy to come on to me, and none of them is aware of any of the others.

L.M., Bakersfield, Calif.

◆ Shower to Shower ◆

Louise and I grew up together; we were next-door neighbors. A lot of people in town thought that we would someday get married. We probably would have if I hadn't been gay. But I like men—what can I say?

When Louise got engaged, she wanted me to meet her fiancé. Ben was a good-looking guy but not really my type. He had reddish-brown hair, which was beginning to thin a little. The rest of his body was very hairy. He also worked out daily, so he had a good build, but he was only 5 feet 6 inches tall.

When Louise's sister gave her a bridal shower, it was my job to get Ben out of the house for the day. We took our bikes and rode along Lake Shore Drive. It was a sunny day when we started out, but the weather in Chicago can change very quickly, and by the time we were halfway back, it started to pour. Since the nearest place to go was Ben's apartment, we headed there.

When we arrived, Ben decided that he was going to take a quick shower. I had started to dry myself off when Ben called out that he needed some soap from the hall closet. I brought it to him, and he pulled open the shower curtain and reached out to grab it.

His body was much better-looking without clothes. As I said, Ben wasn't really my type, but after a quick glance at his well-muscled body, I knew I could very easily make him my type.

As I stood there, almost drooling, he laughed a little and said that it was true what Louise had said about me. Still somewhat disoriented, I asked him what he meant.

With that, he leaned over and slid his tongue down my throat. The one thing that can turn me on instantly is a man who knows how to kiss—and this man knew how. When he asked me if I wanted to help him wash his back, I didn't hesitate.

As I soaped up his lats, I let my tongue move down to the firmest ass I have ever had the pleasure of eating. Ben had no tan line, and the hair on his ass was bleached almost blond by the sun. He tasted so good, bent over, the shower water running down his back and onto my face.

I went from eating out his ass to sucking on his dick. It wasn't the biggest one I'd ever seen—I don't like them too large anyway—but it was the most perfect. As I sucked on his dick, I massaged that beautiful ass of his. When I stuck my finger up his hole, I got a mouthful of come. It was just like finding a hidden treasure.

Thinking that this was just a onetime fling before his wedding, I started to get out of the shower. But Ben blocked my way and asked me where the hell I thought I was going. He then dropped to his knees and proceeded to give me the best blow job I'd ever had. He sucked so hard, my knees almost gave out.

When I came, he kept a little of it in his mouth, stood up, and kissed me so we could both share it.

Louise thinks it's great that her husband and best friend have become close. Ben and I still go bike riding, and we still take a shower together when we're done, but things have changed a bit. Ben and I shower at my condo. Sometimes we even get a chance to ride our bikes.

F.W., Chicago, Ill.

◆ Under Cover of Darkness ◆

Eric and I met during the after-pledge party at our new fraternity. Although I was a freshman and he was a sophomore, we had pledged at the same time. Throughout the next semester, our friendship grew, until I started feeling that I was in love with him. Sometimes I thought that he felt the same way about me but that he was not able to associate feelings of love with another man. That was OK, though, because as I pretty much knew I was gay, I also pretty much knew he was straight.

Over time our friendship progressed, and we became roommates the following year. Our fraternity had a strict policy that all of the new pledges had to live in the house for their first active year. It helped promote unity among the pledge classes and ensured that the house would be full for the year.

I was delighted to share a room with Eric. My roommate the year before was a great guy, and we got along very well, but, physically, he was kind of a dud. He had grown up in a small town and had spent 12 years in a Catholic boys' school. I never once saw him without a shirt, let alone naked. Every night he would get ready for bed in the bathroom we shared with the room next door, and he would emerge wearing the P.E. uniform from his high school. Talk about a prude! Eric, on the other hand, was just my type: A few inches taller than my 5 foot 6, he had a good build and was slightly stocky and very hairy. He had deep brown eyes, framed by long lashes, and dimples that showed up only when he smiled.

As we settled into our new apartment, with two other brothers in the second bedroom, we began to get even closer. At night, watching TV, one of us would recline with the other's head in his lap, slowly stroking the hair on his head. Other times we would carpool home together on weekends (we were from the same city) and hold hands in the car while driving. When I think back on that relationship, I suspect he could be considered my first boyfriend, although at the time neither of us knew what our relationship meant in terms of labels.

Of course, being 19 and 20, we were also at the mercy of our hormones. I had been beating off at least twice a day since I was about 11 or 12, and the fact that someone else was now in my room was not enough to stop me. Apparently it was not enough to stop Eric, either. I would hear the furtive rustling in his bed across the small room each night and know that he was matching me stroke for stroke. Just knowing that he was less than ten feet away from me, touching himself in the same places I was, was enough to make me explode in orgasm. Of course, my explosions were more like implosions because I tried to be as quiet as possible. To this day I have no idea why I tried to hide it like that. It wasn't like he was my mom or anything or that he wasn't doing the exact same thing.

One Sunday afternoon, driving from home back to school, we were chatting away in the car. For some reason the conversation turned to masturbation, and for the first time we found ourselves confessing not only that we did it at the same time in the same room but also that he heard me as often as I heard him! I was astounded (not to mention turned on) and said, "Eric, do you realize that we've been beating off together for months now?"

He replied in the affirmative and began to ask me a few questions.

"How long have you been doing it?" he asked, bright red in the face.

"Since I figured out what it was for," I answered, laughing. "How 'bout you?"

"Well, I knew when I was younger that touching it felt good, but I didn't start coming until later. I was always scared that I would go too far and hurt myself. Then one day I went too far and realized that if what I was feeling was the pain of breaking something, I was going to lead a very painful existence."

We both laughed at that, and then he asked me about technique.

"Do you like rubbing or grasping?"

"When I started, I thought that rubbing was all there was. Then I saw a movie or something, and I tried it with my hand wrapped around my dick, and it felt so much better. How about you?"

"Well," he said shyly, "I like the grasping way, but I also like to play with my perineum. It's kind of hairy, and it feels good to rub it and tug on the hairs when I'm coming."

"Yeah, I know what you mean! I love to pull on the hairs on my balls. Not too hard, just enough to let them know you're there. It feels so good to roll them around in your fingers when you're coming!"

Suddenly Eric looked puzzled. "What do you do with yours when you're done?" he asked.

"My what?"

"Your come. Where does it go? I've looked the next morning, but I've never seen a towel or anything, and you sleep naked. Do you just let it dry?"

"No. I take a sock, stick my dick inside, like I was fucking it, and rub up and down. My dick is cut really tight, and there's no loose skin to move along the shaft, so not only does this give me a quick cleanup, it also provides some welcome friction."

"I get it. I just use my underwear."

"I know. You get into bed wearing them every night, and every morning they're on the floor next to your bed."

"I didn't think you noticed that!"

"Believe me, I did"!

We pulled up to our fraternity house at that moment, and we could see that there was a pledge activity about to take place, so our talk was scrapped for then. But you had better believe that I was going to bring it up later that night. For now I just wanted to get inside, get unpacked, and deal with the pledges.

When we got inside we played our messages and found that our other roommates were having car trouble and would not be back until the following day. The current pledge activity wouldn't take more than an hour, and when it was finished we'd be free for dinner, TV, and then bed. I couldn't wait for bed!

That night, after a couple of joints and some bad sitcoms, we decided to retire at the same time. Eric was the first to bring up our earlier topic.

"Are we going to do what we were talking about?" he asked, his voice almost squeaking.

"I thought we were. Is it still cool?"

"It is with me. Is it cool with you?"

"Yeah." I breathed a sigh of relief. I had almost thought that he was going to chicken out.

All the time we were talking, we were undressing and getting ready for bed. Eric got into his bed first, and as I got into mine, I looked over at him. I could not believe what I was seeing: The light was still on, and he was looking straight at me. The incredible thing was that there was some serious motion going on under the covers in the vicinity of his midsection. I was sitting in my bed, actually watching him masturbate under the covers, when suddenly he pulled the covers over his head, hissing as he shot his load. I was so turned on, I didn't know what to do. He pulled the covers off his face and smiled shyly at me. I did the only thing I could do: I reached down, grabbed myself, and within ten strokes I came too. With Eric watching, I had an orgasm.

After that night our sessions were never that explicit. In fact, they were just like they had been before: in the dark, sound effects only. We modified it, though, creating a code to check our activities with each other. A snap on the band of your underwear meant that you were up for some "action." We would start off together, and eventually one would rest while listening to the other, and vice versa. Usually we would end up coming at roughly the same time.

One night, when Eric had seemed noisier than usual, I asked if he wanted any help with anything. After about ten seconds he said, in a muffled voice, that he could not do anything there at the house. Somewhere else, maybe, but not with the risk of being caught by the other brothers. I never brought up anything like that again—after all, I was quite content with the way things were.

I saw Eric's naked hard dick only once. When I had left for class one morning, he was still in bed. About a block from the house, I realized that I had forgotten something, so I went back. The shower was running, and the bathroom door was ajar. I looked in to see Eric standing on the scale, his morning wood jutting out in front of him. I got what I needed and left, fearful that if he knew I had seen him, he might think that it had been a setup or something.

Things went on the same way for the rest of the year. Eric wanted me to room with him again after that, and it would have been great, but I'd had enough of the frat house. Living with 32 other college guys might sound like fun, but just try it. The drawbacks eventually outweigh the benefits.

Eric and I saw each other very little in the few years after he graduated—only once, in fact, and that was at his wedding. The next time we ran into each other was at our fraternity's ten-year reunion. By then I had been officially out for a while, and everybody in the house knew. There was no question about it; in fact, it was my brothers who supported me most when I came out, even introducing me to guys they thought I would like!

Eric and I saw each other from down the street that night and greeted each other with big hugs. We were virtually inseparable for the rest of the evening, just like we'd been in school. At dinner he said he had a secret to tell me.

"What is it?" I asked, wondering if he was going to come out to me.

"Well, I got my dick pierced."

"What?" I almost shouted. Here I was with the tattoos, the formerly pierced nipple, the ten holes in my ears. I'd never have thought that quiet, shy Eric would do something that wild. "I have to see it," I told him.

"I can't show you here," he said.

"We can go into the bathroom and lock the door."

"I don't know about that..."

"Oh, come on. You can't bring up something like that and then not show me. Besides, it's not like I've never seen it before."

He looked me in the eyes for a long moment and said, "You're right. Let's go."

Eric led me into the bathroom and locked the door. He unzipped his pants and pulled his dick out. It looked just like I remembered it, except now he had a metal bar going right through the underside of it, right below the head. After a short examination we looked at each other and smiled, he zipped up, and we went back to the banquet.

Eric and his wife now live just a couple of miles away from my lover and me. The four of us go out for dinner and have a great time together. I know from the nature of our relationships with our spouses that what we had in college is long gone, but it's definitely not forgotten by either one of us. Every now and then Eric will make some comment and look at me. When he does, the look is as loud as the snap of an underwear waistband.

I.F., Los Angeles, Calif.

◆ Unrequited Love ◆

Even though we had known each other only a few months, I always felt that our friendship was warm and familiar. He knew so much about me: from my simple likes and dislikes to the complexity of my sexuality—of my *homo*sexuality.

"I'm just not attracted to men—or to too many people in general, for that matter," he had said in the beginning.

Every night we would have long conversations, and then we would each retire—alone—to our separate rooms. I was saddened but also proud that we maintained this progressive, honest relationship—this brotherhood—and was happy that we understood the boundaries of friendship despite the irony of our bond.

His upper body was large and muscular. When he spoke to me, I would watch his mouth move, gazing at his full lips. It never got me hard, but thinking of him made my mouth water. At those times it was hard not to remember all the gray areas of our friendship.

Sometimes at night I would dream of being on top of him, fucking his tight hole or biting his hard neck. I could have told him this, and nothing would have changed between us. But I did not.

He drank once in a while, and on those nights he would stumble into the apartment to tell me his secrets. Our eyes might lock for a moment, and then we would turn away, embarrassed, like children.

I wanted to be clear about my feelings. Never did I want to be the stereotypical homo chasing after the straight boy, but the love I felt for him was pure.

For me, the occasional fantasies I had seemed healthy, but even as I held firm to the limits I had set, the boundaries for him seemed to lift.

At times I noticed his looking at me like I was a stranger. Sometimes he would cut our conversations short as if I had offended him. He would feign exhaustion and walk out of the room, always leaving me wanting more of him, wanting to pull him back, push him against the wall, and press my weight against his frame.

I would imagine his turning his head away from me. I would grab the back of his neck and kiss his face, licking it as though we were animals. He would protest, just to hear the sound of his voice, but he would not really make an effort to break free. Our hard cocks would press together, and my hot balls would rest against his thighs, which were muscular yet smooth as silk.

While I lost myself in my dreams, I would always be awakened by his voice saying good night. Then I'd be left alone to hear him, awake, in his room for hours afterward.

I had decided that if we ever did have sex, it would be at his request. He might whisper in my ear, "Fuck me, I want to feel you inside me."

I would think about this as I listened to him masturbate behind the wall that separated us. Hearing his bed shake rhythmically, I would wonder what he was thinking, wonder about the expression on his face as he held that fat dick in his hand and stroked it. Did he finger his hot ass and think of me?

In the daylight it was back to business as usual. Thoughts of his thighs against my chest or his feet locked behind my head vanished with the dark sky. But I knew I wanted to be the one to show him at some point in time what it felt like to be locked together in that kind of heat.

As we sat drinking our coffee that morning, it occurred to me that years had passed. We had had our lovers and friends. We had traveled together to the mountains and the shore. If we were to become lovers, there would be no need for anyone else. How dangerous it was that we fit together like pieces to a puzzle. If the only distance between us was sexual and we could bridge that gap, we would possess the thing everyone constantly claims to want. Are our wishes our fears? Finally, I was the one who put down my coffee cup and left the room.

D.S., Montclair, N.J.

◆ Usual Suspects ◆

This happened last October on an unusually warm evening. I had returned to school as a full-time student to complete my master's degree in computer science. In doing so, I had taken on the typical student schedule of long nights and late mornings. This particular incident happened during one of those late-night vigils at the keyboard of my computer.

I was deep in thought, totally unaware of anything around me. Suddenly my thoughts were shattered by a loud knock on the door. It was after 2 a.m., and I had no idea who could be visiting me so late.

Anxious to get my work finished, I ignored whoever it was and turned back to my work. But a few minutes later the doorbell started ringing constantly; this person obviously wasn't going to go away.

I went to the door, wearing nothing but my skimpy briefs. The weather was extremely hot, and I figured whoever was rude enough to come calling at such a late hour didn't deserve any manners. Right before I opened it, though, I threw on a pair of jeans.

The ringing persisted. Hesitantly I opened the door and found two policemen lurking in the shadows outside. From what I could see in the darkness, one was quite handsome.

He looked Italian. He had a slightly balding head of jet-black hair, and he appeared to be in his early 30s. His scruffy five-o'clock shadow showed the promise of a full beard, and he wore a thick black mustache that had flecks of gray in it.

It was also clear that he worked out on a regular basis. His shirt collar was unbuttoned, with his tie slightly askew. Black chest hair curled around the tie. Hairy guys have always turned me on, and this guy looked like the man of my dreams.

The other cop was older and obviously had worked long and hard to develop his beer belly. What little hair he had left on his head was reddish white. He was the senior officer and wanted to make that perfectly clear from the beginning. "We're looking for a Lou Carls," he grumbled through the doorway.

"He moved out last month," I replied sharply. "Besides, he lived in the front apartment." I was pissed at having been disturbed so late just because this guy didn't check his facts. I started to shut the door but was stopped midway by a foot stuck in the jamb.

"Mind if we have a look around? Just to check?"

Before I had a chance to say, "Yes, I do mind," he barged past me and into my apartment. I trailed behind helplessly, and the other cop followed me. The young hairy one introduced himself as Joe and the other cop as Tim. Tim was busy poking around in the cupboards; I had no idea what—or whom—he expected to find in there.

"Sorry about this," Joe whispered. "Tim takes his work a little too seriously."

"That's an understatement," I replied snidely.

Tim headed for my bedroom. "Do you mind?" I hollered as I saw him rummaging through my dresser drawers. "Do you have a warrant?"

Tim ignored me. "Hey, what's this?" he called out. "Looks like we have something interesting here."

Tim had stumbled upon my rather extensive collection of gay porn magazines. It obviously didn't please him. Suddenly he got a strange look in his eye; I could almost read his thoughts. Then in one full swoop Tim was on top of me. He slapped a pair of handcuffs on one of my wrists and attached the other to the bedpost.

"Come on, Joe," he urged the cute officer. "Give me your cuffs."

Joe hesitated for a moment, but Tim insisted. Soon my other arm was cuffed to the bed: My feet were free, though, and I used them for all they were worth. I kicked up at Tim and hit him with a considerable amount of force—square in the balls.

He doubled over in pain. "You'll be sorry you did that," he warned. I already was.

Tim went and got some rope from the patrol car and cut

it in half. Then he tied my legs firmly to the bedposts at the foot of the bed.

"Now, let's have a little fun," he sneered at me.

Tim unzipped his uniform pants and pulled out his dick. It was small and shriveled but not that bad to look at. He climbed on the bed and straddled my head.

His prick was beginning to get hard, growing quickly into a nice fat specimen. He put it up to my mouth and cooed, "Suck it real nice and easy. Any teeth, and you won't have any left to use."

I tried to hold my mouth locked shut, but Tim kneed me in the nuts and pried my mouth open. He stuck his dick in, and I gagged from the sheer size of it. I sucked hard, trying to get him off quickly so I could move on to Joe. The whole time, Joe stood off to one side, sulking and looking pretty embarrassed.

I could tell it wouldn't take much to get Tim off. His balls were already heaving up toward his body.

"Take it easy," he said. "I'm not ready to come yet." He pulled his cock out of my mouth—thank God!—and climbed off me. "Go ahead, Joe, your turn."

Joe didn't seem to want to do it, but with a little more prodding he was soon standing naked at the foot of the bed. He was a great-looking man. His body was hard and tight, with not an ounce of fat anywhere. His limp cock was about seven inches long, with a nice piece of foreskin covering its head. I was silently wishing that Joe would get down to business.

He climbed onto the bed and got into position to fuck my mouth, then began to pump it with a good fucking motion.

He was showing much more care for me, and, to be honest, I was really enjoying it.

I knew I was giving him a hell of a blow job; from the expression on his face, I could tell he was loving it as much as I was. I watched the heaving of his broad, hairy chest as he pumped into my mouth. I wrapped my tongue around his hard shaft and slid my mouth up and down, doing as good a job as I could considering that I was so well-restrained. It was becoming rather obvious that I was enjoying this too: My dick was getting hard.

Suddenly, out of the corner of my eye, I noticed a look of disgust on Tim's face. He saw that Joe and I were getting into each other, and he couldn't stand it. I was so happy when he stormed out the front door. Once he was gone, Joe loosened the binds and set my arms and legs free. Then he gave me a slow massage to get my circulation going again. He was so gentle and seemed so experienced, I would have never guessed it was his first time.

Lying full on top of me, he pressed our cocks together and then dry-humped me between my thighs. His strong tool pumped insistently, forcing my legs apart, and then he rubbed the whole length of his shaft over my ball sac.

It didn't take me long to come with prodding like that. I shot a small but incredibly satisfying load all over my belly. It mashed between our bodies, gluing us together.

Then Joe lifted my legs over his shoulders and cooed in my ear. He said that he would be gentle and that I should try to relax.

He gently slid his cock into my ass. It was obvious that he was more interested in making love to me than fucking me. He slowly pumped my ass as he gently caressed my chest and nuzzled my neck.

I relaxed my muscles so he could pump a little harder. I could feel the thick black bush at the base of his cock brushing against my crack, and it was making me hot all over again. With every stroke Joe's big, fat, hairy balls slapped my ass cheeks. His cock swelled to its full size in my body, and I could tell that he was close to coming.

Joe placed his entire weight on top of me and slowed down his pace. He was now gently rocking back and forth on top of me. His arms were wrapped firmly around my chest, with his hands busily massaging and fondling my nipples. I could feel the thick hair on his chest against my back. His tongue darted up and down my neck, sending chills down my spine. Then he shot inside my ass, covering my insides with his hot, milky jizz.

With a quick kiss and a slap on my ass, he was gone.

L.S., Poughkeepsie, N.Y.

◆ Vacation Education ◆

I had rented the cottage for a summer getaway and, tired of preparing my own means, was headed for the restaurant down the beach. As I returned, the skies opened up in a torrential downpour, drenching everything. It was then that I regretted walking the half mile to dinner instead of taking the car.

As I neared my cottage, I found Tom, whom I had met on the lake a few days earlier, slouched on a bench by the dock. It was obvious that he had been drinking and had passed out because even the cold September rain hadn't wakened him.

Tom and his wife had a cottage up the beach from mine. It was too late to try to get him home, so I decided to get him up to my place, which was only a few yards away. Tom was heavy, the result of years of weight lifting, so I was exhausted by the time I got him inside and out of his wet clothes in front of a roaring fire.

I had never been attracted to another man before, but seeing his tight, muscular body lying naked in the flickering firelight was strangely stimulating. Perhaps it was the thick uncut cock standing straight up through his dense bush. His cock wasn't hard; it just naturally stuck straight out. The only hair he had was on his chest and at the base of his cock. Getting up to get him a blanket, I realized that I was hard myself, and I was glad Tom was still asleep and unable to notice.

Dawn arrived all too early, and I awoke to find Tom making breakfast. He was still naked, and I couldn't help observing what perfect shape he was in and how round and firm his butt was. I was desperately trying not to examine him in such a manner, but his flawless physique made it impossible.

He thanked me for last night and apologized for not wearing anything; he couldn't find his clothes, which were still in a sodden pile on the front porch. Bringing the clothes in, I told him it looked like it would be a while longer before they were dry and that he'd be welcome to stay until then.

As Tom served us breakfast, I found myself watching his every move. It wasn't long before he asked why I was staring at him. I tried to deny it, but he was adamant. I finally made a flimsy excuse about being happy to have company for the first time on my vacation.

As we ate and talked, I felt his foot playing with mine under the table. Then, as we finished, I felt his toes gently pushing against my crotch. Jumping to his feet, Tom said, "It's time for the dishes." Embarrassed by my rising prick, I tried to use the table for concealment, but Tom pulled me away from the table, exposing my woody.

He smiled and said, "Looks like the dishes will have to wait." Taking my hand and leading me to the bedroom, he guided me to the bed and sat down facing me, our legs stretched out around each other. As he pulled me close, I could feel the warmth emanating from his body, his breath tickling the hairs on my chest. He gently grabbed my cock with one hand and peeled back his foreskin with the other, then placed my hands against his and wrapped his extensive overhang around the head of my cock. It felt so fantastic, so warm, its tightness squeezing my cock, that I soon lost my inhibitions. I grabbed his cock and tugged downward, watching his glans pop from its prison. Wet with sweat, it smelled sweet, and I leaned forward to examine it more closely.

Aware of my inexperience, Tom was eager to show me the ropes and quickly flipped around into a sixty-nine position and buried his head in my crotch. I had only to follow his lead. I teased his balls with my tongue while gently stroking his cock with my hand. He swallowed my prick, and I followed suit with his, probing my tongue into his foreskin.

It wasn't long before I was able to devour his whole cock. By then he was moaning and groaning, pleading for release, the veins in his cock protruding under the pressure of his need to come. Spitting on my hand, I grabbed his dick and started pumping, slowly at first, then fast and hard.

His toes curled, and he went into a sex-driven fit, thrashing uncontrollably. His juices shot quickly, coating us both, and seconds later I came too.

As he left, Tom told me I'd have to do some shaving before next time, that it was much more exhilarating to suck hairless balls. Smiling, I said I'd definitely need some help shaving that area.

Two days later Tom showed up at the door with a razor in his hand and a huge bulge in his pants…but that's Part 2 of my vacation.

D.W., London, Canada

◆ Vintage Hardball ◆

Someone in the Cannonballs' marketing and promotion department came up with the bright idea of having the team dress in vintage circa-1900s uniforms to kick off the second half of the big-league baseball season. It all sounded good on paper, but try getting 27 guys and their coaches to play hard and sweaty in high-80–heat index weather with something made out of wool on their backs, and you can pretty much imagine the problems. To most of us, though, baseball was life, so we did it.

Our team clown was a big crew-cut veteran named Mark. Mark didn't mind the dark blue baseball shirts and pantaloons that showed sanitary sweat socks as high as the knees or the fact that modern-day batting helmets, footgear, batting gloves, shin and elbow guards didn't match the old team duds; the old team uniforms were one more opportunity to tease the new rookies who didn't know the full extent of Mark's reputation as the clubhouse comedian. One of those new guys was me. And the fact that bat day—when the first 10,000 fans were given free miniature autographed lumber—had occurred the week before the All-Star break gave him a perfect chance to dupe us.

There was only one problem. Mark hadn't anticipated how much I secretly jonesed on him.

Sure, sex between guys happens in the major leagues, just like it does everywhere else. But it's kept more secret than signs, so when Mark came up to me and shoved what I thought was his hard cock against my ass in the middle of batting practice the day of the vintage hardball game, right in front of a whole bunch of our team members, I nearly jumped out of my cleats.

"You look *real* sweet," Mark said, his voice a seductive growl. I whipped around to see that he had one of those 12-inch miniature bats hanging out of the front of his vintage pants, with the handle zipped in at an angle to make it look like he'd popped a rock-hard dick out of his fly. "Oh, rookie, I think I'm in *love!*"

All the guys started laughing, just like Mark had wanted. But me—I'm pretty fast on my feet, which is why I bat second. I reached around and gave the bat a good, hard punch that sent the handle drumming into his cup. A breathless "*Ungh!*" sounded over my shoulder. Mark let out a good-natured "Asshole!" then pulled out the mini bat and handed it to me. "A token of my love, boy."

Everything was cool after that. Mark picked up his lumber, rubbed pine tar onto the handle, and assumed the stance in the batting cage. He was something to look at, the way he swung his bat, how every muscle in his body was so perfect. From head to toe and everywhere in between, even in the old vintage unis, he was a baseball god, and secretly I would have loved to have felt his real cock sticking out of his pants against me. But as bad as Mark had tried to embarrass me, nothing was worse than the fact that he'd made me pop a bat of my own in my cup, and as hard as I tried to get it to go down, it wouldn't. I stayed half stiff through the next four hours. Hell, we lost the game on national TV. Worse, I had Mark's first-base butt in front of me from my position in right field the whole time. It was there, as I was staring at the sweat-soaked square of his hard jock ass, that I came up with a plan to get Mark back—and maybe, just maybe, get Mark.

It's always somber in the locker room after a loss. This time was no different. As the guys peeled off their hot, dirty wool unis and paraded into the showers, I saw Mark sitting alone, down near his locker, unlacing his cleats. Since the media loves winners and rarely talks to the losers, our locker room was pretty empty, and the showers were strictly off-limits to all but the players, so I pretty much had Mark to myself.

"*Hey,*" I growled in a cocky voice as I approached him, dressed only in my jock.

Two wounded baby-blues looked up. "Hey, yourself, rookie." I clapped Mark's shoulder and arched a leg up onto the bench beside him. He was shucking his sweat socks when he said, "What do you want?"

I glanced around, sure that no one was within earshot.

"That was a pretty funny stunt you pulled on me during batting practice earlier."

"Rookies gotta be able to take it. That's the law."

"Oh, I can take it, man," I said. "You man enough to give it—I mean *really* give it?"

Mark stood up and pushed down his pants, leaving him dressed only in his jockstrap. As he fished out the cup, letting his perspiration-drenched balls hang openly, I sat on the bench beside him. Mark let out a deep, confident chuckle. "What the fuck are you talking about?"

"That bat you tried shoving up my ass…" Boldly I put a hand on the hairy muscles of his thigh. Mark flinched, but not before I took hold of his fat, sweaty nuts, giving them a firm squeeze that seemed to deflate any protest he was going to make. Mark's hot, heavy sac caused the lump in my jock to push painfully against the cup. But then, just as suddenly as I did it, I let go of his meat and left him sitting there, openmouthed, a dazed look on his face. I'd gotten my payback!

By the time I hit the showers, I figured I was the last guy to hose down—the last except for Mark. I don't think I was in the steam two seconds before I heard the sound of big feet in a pair of shower flip-flops entering. Then something landed with a crash on the tiles below me. I looked down to see a bar of soap. I laughed as Mark came right up into the spray beside me.

"So, fucker," he growled, "are you man enough to take the real thing?"

I knew I'd *finally* bagged him, even before I caught a glimpse of his naked lumber, all fat in the middle with its long, rounded head stretched to full mast, those same sweat-soaked balls hanging low beneath it.

"More of a man than it'll take to choke up on *that.*"

I stared the veteran slugger head-on, saw the intensity in his deep blue eyes, before gripping his bat by its hairy handle. I felt Mark tense up. I could tell it had to do with losing the game as well as being squeezed by a teammate. He groaned in my ear as I strummed on his wood from its handle up to the head.

"I'm starting to respect the rookies on this team more and more..."

From there I got down on my knees like the team's catcher and sucked his cock between my goatee and mustache, taking most of the shaft down my throat. Mark let out a manly growl as I toyed with his low-hangers, rolling the hairy sac over my nose and face. Luckily, the clean, hot spray hadn't yet washed out all of his man sweat, so after a few good hits of his bat, I moved down to his nuts, sucking the left, then spitting it out and going on to his right. His balls tasted like the game—hot and aggressive, powerful and pure. After cleaning his bag of a hard nine innings, I got back to Mark's bat and choked up, putting both hands on his rock-solid outer thighs to steady myself. He charged on, fucking my face with the kind of jock intensity only an athlete can muster.

"Take it, fucker!" he huffed, pushing in harder and harder. Mark's cock ran over my tongue and plunged down my throat. The next time he rammed in, I ran my hands over his hairy ass cheeks, spreading them enough to tease the tight, bullet-proof hole in his crack. It was full of hair and sweat, but I wormed my fuck finger in, right up to the second knuckle. Mark groaned and shoved his bat in again. This time, when he pulled back, I got my first shock of salt to the tongue. The heavy, musky taste of Mark's precome caused the hard-on swinging between my own legs to spring up to its full eight inches. With Mark dribbling and fucking my face and me fingering his asshole, that's how I thought we'd both shoot our tar. But just as I started paddling my own bat, Mark ripped his out of my mouth, leaving a trail of salty goo on my tongue.

"No way, fucker, you ain't getting my juice in your mouth," Mark said, a mean smirk on his face when I looked up. "Pick up that bar of soap."

I sent back a smirk of my own and retrieved the bar of soap from where it lay on the drain and handed it to him.

"Time to teach the rookie some respect..."

The moment Mark had the soap in his big mitt, he pulled me up to my feet and spun me around. I'd already learned the position during my college varsity days, so I got down on my haunches, baring my shitter for him to mount. I felt the bar of soap as he worked it into my crack, then Mark assumed his stance behind me and aimed his bat at my slick rookie's hole. He pushed in. *Home run!*

The size of his massive cock and the pressure in my gut caused me to see stars. He shoved his bat all the way in, until our bodies were pressed together in the spray. One of Mark's arms gripped my abs. The other went around my chest. He started to fuck me slowly at first, then faster and faster as I played with my own cock. Soon my pain turned to pleasure.

"You got a hot ass, rookie," he growled into my ears. His breath, hot and heavy with the smell of bubble gum, blasted against my neck as he plowed my ass. I felt Mark's meaty balls banging against the bottom of my can, and I knew it wouldn't be long for either of us, especially since we didn't want to be caught by our teammates.

Mark's pent-up aggression from having lost the game was being taken out on my shitter. He shoved in one last time, let out a muffled howl, and squirted me full of come. I shot my foam into the drain.

"Fuckin' rookies," he groaned before pulling his dick out. "Thanks…"

Then he kissed me.

We showered together side by side. It was as if I'd been initiated into the veteran's circle and now had the respect of the big ballplayer. And while Mark's jokes and pranks continued for the rest of the season, so did the sex.

Next year was *my* turn to "break in" the new rookies.

G.N., Atkinson, N.H.